The report came uown
was giving him at   d of
the target and th   tion
that would have   got?'
Nasmith asked h

'Forty-five fat

They were al   l just
started to zig-zag away   wards
the target now. You keep your eyes glued on that destroyer, and
tell me if she alters course.' He sent the look-out below, and went
to the voice-pipe, 'Group up! Full power! Starboard ten ...
Steady. Keep her steady now!' In one minute he would be in
position to launch his torpedo. 'Full fields! Stand by now ...'

'Destroyer swinging, sir!' Brown sang out. 'Destroyer altering towards. Heading straight for us, sir! Three hundred yards
... Two hundred yards ...'

'Get below!' Nasmith shouted, and sounded the klaxon.
'Group up! Full ahead both! Fifty feet! Take her down quick!'

He had a glimpse of the sharp bows of the destroyer cutting
through the sea, and the spray shooting out on each side, and he
leapt down the hatch after Brown, pulling the lid shut and
securing it after him ...

PETER SHANKLAND
and
ANTHONY HUNTER

Dardanelles Patrol

GRANADA
London Toronto Sydney New York

Published by Granada Publishing Limited in 1971
Reprinted 1971, 1978, 1983

ISBN 0 583 11861 5

First published in Great Britain by
William Collins 1964
Copyright © Peter Shankland and Anthony Hunter 1964

Granada Publishing Limited
Frogmore, St Albans, Herts AL2 2NF
and
36 Golden Square, London W1R 4AH
515 Madison Avenue, New York, NY 10022, USA
117 York Street, Sydney, NSW 2000, Australia
60 International Blvd, Rexdale, Ontario R9W 6J2, Canada
61 Beach Road, Auckland, New Zealand

Printed and bound in Great Britain by
Cox & Wyman Ltd, Reading
Set in Monotype Plantin

Granada ®
Granada Publishing ®

The Naval History of Britain contains no page more wonderful than that which records the prowess of her submarines at the Dardanelles.

WINSTON CHURCHILL

ACKNOWLEDGEMENTS

We wish to express our particular thanks to Admiral Sir Martin Dunbar-Nasmith, V.C., for his kindness in putting his records, his memory and his time at our disposal. Without his co-operation the book could not have been written. We also wish to express our thanks to Admiral C. G. Brodie for permission to use material from his book *Forlorn Hope–1915* (W. J. Bryce, Ltd., 1956) and for many helpful suggestions; to Captain H. G. Stoker, D.S.O., for allowing us to draw on his book *Straws in the Wind* (Herbert Jenkins, Ltd., 1925); and to Mrs. D'Oyly Hughes for her reminiscences. We were fortunate in being able to contact several members of E 11's crew, and we are grateful to them for their eye-witness accounts – particularly to Reginald Jupp, D.S.M., William Wheeler, D.S.M., George Plowman, D.S.M., Ernest Baker, D.S.M., David Greene, D.S.M., and Bertram Cornish, D.S.M. Finally we have, once again, to record our appreciation of the help we have received from the Admiralty, the Public Record Office and the Imperial War Museum.

The Sea of Marmara
and its approaches

To Adriane

T U R K E Y

RODOSTO

Panidos

Kodja Bu

Xeros Island

H.M.S. JED

GULF of XEROS

Bulair   30 mile
                W/T range

GALLIPOLI PENINSULA

GALLIPOLI

GALLIPOLI STRAIT W/T range

30 mile
W/T range

Suvla
Bay

GALLIPOLI

Burgaz

GU
A

Kilia
Bahr

The
Narrows

Cape
Helles
DARDANELLES

Kum Kale

T U R K E Y

0   10   20   30   40   50 mile

The Dardanelles
with inset map showing
their relationship to the
Eastern Mediterranean

ooooo   Mine fields
⟩   Heavy gun emplacement
·   Light gun emplacement
(The numerals denote the number of guns)
⟨   Searchlights
≡≡≡   Held by the Allies

Suvla
Bay

Gapa
Tepe

Nagara

Kilid
Bahr

Chemenlik

Chanak

Suan Dere

Achi Baba

Kephez Pt.

Seddul
Bahr

Cape
Helles

Kum Kale

Orkanieh

0   5   10 miles

12

Details not known of the enemy defences above the Narrows

GALLIPOLI

Chardak Liman

Karakova Burnu

Lampsaki

Kudjuk Burnu

Moussa Bank

Burgaz

ITALY

SERBIA BULGARIA

Constantinople

ALBANIA

GREECE

OTTOMAN EMPIRE

CYPRUS

13

On the morning of the 29th of March, 1915, with the wind northwest and the barometer falling, the submarine depot ship *Adamant* and three of Britain's newest submarines, E 14, E 15 and E 11, were steering south across the Bay of Biscay in line ahead with *Adamant* leading. There was nothing else in sight in the vast expanse of long green rollers streaked with white under a grey sky. *Adamant,* resembling a large steam yacht, rolled heavily, showing the red anti-fouling paint below her waterline, in spite of a small foresail to steady her. Her only means of defence was a dummy gun made of an old stove pipe that would look menacing to a U Boat, as real guns were in short supply. The three submarines, identical in design, pitched and rolled with a livelier movement. Lieutenant-Commander Nasmith, captain of E 11, bringing up the rear, stood on the diminutive bridge on the conning tower beside the stolid helmsman, and gave orders through the voice-pipe to the engine-room to increase or decrease the revolutions of the propellers to keep station on E 15. He wore a chauffeur's long leather coat, a uniform cap, muffler and sea-boots. Every now and again the hissing crest of a sea, approaching from the starboard quarter, swept over the long, narrow grey-green superstructure, foamed round the base of the conning tower and then receded to show the top of the dark bulging cylinder of the pressure hull beneath.

After months of patrolling off Heligoland and the Jahde Estuary watching ceaselessly for the German fleet to come out, they had left their base at Harwich on the morning of the 27th to join the East Mediterranean Fleet now concentrated off the entrance of the Dardanelles.

Nasmith was a powerful, compact figure of medium height with cheerful weather-beaten features and decisive movements. In peacetime he had been Chief Instructor in underwater tactics. Under his guidance at Fort Blockhouse, the submarine training base at Portsmouth, the art of attacking with the torpedo, from being an affair of inspired guesswork, had become an exact science. He had also considerable prestige as the inventor of the retractable periscope, and of the range and distance finder in use by the British and United States navies. Consequently, when war broke out and he was given command of E 11, a great deal had been expected of him: but expectations had not been fulfilled. It was a story of breakdowns, accidents, missed opportunities. Even before her trials, the first time she was moved from the builders' fitting-out basin, E 11 had run against a chain hanging from a low bridge and smashed her forward periscope, and there had been trouble of one kind or another ever since. Other captains had already achieved fame by their exploits, while he was known only as one who had miraculously survived a series of near disasters. He felt intensely that this new adventure would play a decisive part in his life. He was leaving the past behind him with all its disappointments and the baffling circumstances which had made every patrol fail of its object, or achieve only partial success; and he was taking with him into the future a crew who would be equal to any demands he made on them, a boat tried and tested in every bolt and rivet, machinery going like clockwork and, above all, his own bitterly gained experience. This time nothing had gone wrong, nothing had delayed him, and his heart was light.

Whenever a shower of spray flew over the bridge, some of it spattered down into the control room through the partly-open conning tower hatch, to be mopped up by a waiting seaman. It was partly open because the heavy diesel engines required an ample supply of air: if it and the ventilators were closed, they would quickly exhaust the air, and the men would be unable to breathe.

The pressure hull of a submarine is shaped like a long narrow tube. The lower part is entirely taken up by tanks, stores, batteries and compressed air bottles: the deck upon which the men stand is half-way up, so headroom is greatly restricted by the curving sides, except in the centre where the curves reach up to form the control room and support the conning tower. The upper part of the tube where the men live and work is a mass of intricate machinery with a passageway in the middle sealed off, section by section, by bulkheads with watertight doors. In E 11 there was no space to sling hammocks, and the men slept whereever they could, among the machinery or on the boards in the central passageway which covered the batteries. The rush of air being sucked through the boat, the horrible moaning sound of the steering gear and the clatter of the engines, made it impossible for a human voice to be heard. The stoker on duty in the engine-room had to strike the steel plates of the deck with a spanner to attract the attention of one of the artificers, and then communicate with him in sign language.

On the third day out, the even rhythm of the engines faltered: they slowed down, back-fired, accelerated and slowed down again. Lieutenant D'Oyly-Hughes, a tall young Northern Irishman who as first lieutenant was in charge of everything down below, hastily pulled on his dungarees and made his way along the slippery heaving alleyway to consult with Jupp, the chief engine-room artificer. They traced the trouble to the fuel oil which they were carrying in the ballast tanks as a reserve supply. Owing to the violent motion of the boat, it had mixed with seawater and become emulsified. Until the weather modified they would only be able to draw on the main fuel tanks.

The only other officer on board was Lieutenant Robert Brown R.N.R. He had no part in the general routine or working of the boat. He was twenty-eight, and had been an officer with an extra-master's ticket in Alfred Holt's Blue Funnel Line. His job while under way was always to know where they were, and he kept a complete record of every course, speed, depth, or any order affecting the position of the boat. He also looked after the navigational instruments. He was popular with the crew – not 'service,' of course like Nasmith, but one of themselves almost, a short, thickset fellow with round smiling face, auburn hair, and a twinkle in his eye that he could not disguise even on the most solemn occasion.

Nasmith on the bridge in his streaming leather coat, watched E 14 and E 15 ahead, sometimes showing on a crest, sometimes disappearing in a trough, and wondered what was in store for them. They both had good skippers – Lieutenant-Commander Boyle in E 14 and Lieutenant-Commander T. S. Brodie in E 15 – but Nasmith was pretty sure that E 11 would be sent on any dangerous mission in preference to the others. He believed that he still had the complete confidence of Commodore Roger Keyes who had been, until recently, at Harwich as Commodore of Submarines, and was now Chief of Staff to the Commander-in-Chief, Eastern Mediterranean, Admiral De Robeck. Neither of his two officers seemed to have any particular curiosity about their destination or what they were going to attempt: for D'Oyly, probably, it was enough that they were off on a new adventure, and for Brown, cool and smiling as usual, it was just another job of work. But Nasmith expected that Keyes would use the submarines in an attempt to force the Dardanelles, the narrow thirty-five mile long Straits dividing Asia from Europe and giving access to the Sea of Marmara on which lay Constantinople, for the battleships had tried to get through and failed.

What were the hazards he would have to face? The highest proportion of all submarine losses were due to mines, and it was certain that the winding treacherous waters of the Straits had been sown thick with them. Only a fortnight ago, on the 18th of March, two British battleships, *Ocean* and *Irresistible,* and the French battleship *Bouvet* had been mined and sunk in the lower reaches, and *Inflexible* badly damaged – but he thought it possible, just possible, that mines fatal to surface vessels might not be fatal to submarines. If he dived deeply below them . . . of course he wouldn't be able to avoid striking their mooring wires, but that shouldn't explode them unless the boat actually fouled a mooring and dragged the mine down on top of her. The risk was a fair one. The detonating horns were on the upper half of the mine, the horns that must be touched before it would explode, and the submarine should be well below, unless the mines had been purposely set deep.

There would be nets perhaps: at home we had had some success in trapping U Boats in nets. With the sharp cutting edge on E 11's bows he would thrash his way through them like a swordfish!

Shore-based guns? There would be many, and at night they would be working with searchlights. When he got too near them he would have to dive, and risk the odd plunging shell. Would there be shore-based torpedo tubes? These might be deadly. He could only pray that the Turks were without them, or without the skill to handle them efficiently. Patrol craft and destroyers? He would dodge them: E 11 should be a match for them as long as the batteries were charged and he could use the motors. . . . That was the crux of the matter. The Admiralty charts he had studied indicated an outflowing current of two to six knots . . . the distance thirty-five miles . . . E 11 couldn't go anything like this distance against the current submerged. At some point on the way up she would have to surface and recharge, but that seemed impossible without being picked up by the searchlights and sunk by gunfire. Of course he would have to push the periscope up every now and again to get his bearings in that narrow twisting channel, at places only three quarters of a mile wide . . . to take bearings on what? Perhaps on the enemy searchlights if their exact position could be plotted – or were they mobile? Perhaps on the contours of the hills, if there was light enough to

18

see them? That seemed the most certain, if one hill could be distinguished from another. If he waited for daylight, he might be attacked not only by guns and patrols, but from the air . . . He had had a nasty few minutes with a zeppelin once in the North Sea while he was picking up the seaplane crews after their unsuccessful attempt to raid the zeppelin sheds at Cuxhaven. It had hovered overhead while he rescued three pilots and two observers, but he had been forced to dive before sinking the planes, as he had been ordered to do, because he sighted another submarine apparently diving to attack him – he discovered later that it was a British submarine out of position. However, the zeppelin, after dropping its bombs close to E 11, sunk the planes for him by machine-gun fire. In a subsequent patrol he had got right in among the German High Seas Fleet, the dream of every submarine commander, but Fate had been against him and he had failed to score a hit. . . . Constantinople would wipe out all the past, the glittering jewel on the Sea of Marmara, the proud harbour into which no enemy had sailed since the Turks conquered it nearly five hundred years ago, preserved inviolate by the thirty-five-mile length of the treacherous Dardanelles.

The wind eased on the afternoon of the 1st of April. As they passed Cape St. Vincent and Sagres, the south-west corner of Portugal, they altered course to eastward towards Gibraltar. The sea was dark blue now, and the sky a lighter grey, but heavy clouds were massing in the east. With Cape St. Vincent dying away to the north-west they passed close to Cape Trafalgar, not "bluish 'mid the burning water" but sombre and dark, echoing to the thunder of breakers in its subterranean caverns and garlanded with sea mist. A French cruiser passed them, heading out into the Atlantic, crashing through the seas on some urgent mission, sending the spray high over her masts. They entered the Straits, keeping over to the African side to get the benefit of the strong inflowing current. At 6.35 that evening they entered the harbour at Gibraltar and made fast to the north mole. The crews of the submarines were transferred to *Adamant* for the night.

They were unable to refuel at Gibraltar as there was no oil available of the grade that they required. Malta, their next port of call, was 1,000 miles away. E 14 and E 15 could make it comfortably on their remaining fuel. Nasmith calculated that E 11 could make it also, although the oil in one of the ballast tanks was now unserviceable, but there would be no margin for accident or bad weather. To add to the difficulty of his decision, Jupp had reported that the star clutch was stiff when they changed over to the electric motors for entering harbour. This was a serious defect. A submarine runs on the surface on her powerful and economical diesel engines, and submerged on electric motors. Before she can dive, the diesels have to be disconnected to allow the electric motors to be operated independently of them. Sometimes this has to be done in a hurry for a crash dive, so it was vital that the clutch should be in perfect order. The electric motors were used also for manœuvring among other shipping, as the diesels could not go astern, and the harbour under the towering Rock was crowded with shipping. D'Oyly and the artificers spent the whole morning testing it, but no reason could be found for it being stiff. The intermediate shaft between the engines and the electric motors seemed to be running smoothly in perfect alignment, so Nasmith decided to risk going on to Malta with the other boats, and they sailed in company during the night of the 3rd of April.

The next day the weather was fair. The sun shone brilliantly. The mountains of Africa rose warm and brown to the south. There was a light breeze and the feel of a Mediterranean summer in the air which was very welcome after a winter spent patrolling in cold mist and rain where long yellow seas break on to the low-lying sandbanks of the German North Sea estuaries. Nasmith had every excuse to remain quietly at Gibraltar until a tanker should arrive from England with the correct fuel – a matter of days, perhaps, or weeks – during which time he could have had his clutch put in order, or replaced, in the naval dockyard, but he was determined not to be left behind. A similar delay, near the beginning of the war, had had unhappy results and lost him a golden opportunity. E 1, E 9 and E 11 had been ordered to get into the Baltic Sea and attack the valuable cargoes of iron ore that were being run between Sweden and the German Baltic ports. It was necessary to pass through the Kattegat, a narrow sound with no deeps to hide in, between Sweden and Denmark. For six miles the sound was so shallow that the submarines would have to bump along the rocky bottom with their conning towers showing. As both countries were known to be winking at the German patrols in their neutral waters, surprise had to be achieved, and it was planned that the three submarines should pass through on the same night of the 17th October with an interval of two hours only between each boat. E 1, commanded by Laurence, and E 9, commanded by Horton, slipped through unobserved, but E 11 was delayed by a serious engine defect. When she attempted the passage, twenty-four hours late, Laurence had attacked a German light cruiser, and the hunt was on. The moment she appeared off the Sound, the inky blackness was stabbed by blinding searchlights and star shells, and she was hunted relentlessly by a succession of seaplanes working with destroyers. Three times she was nearly rammed. She had no chance to lie on the surface to recharge. At last, with batteries exhausted, she had to return to Harwich after the longest patrol on record. Keyes always maintained that the attempt, and particularly the survival, was a brilliant feat – but he had failed to follow Horton and Laurence into the Baltic – that was the point. He had expected to try again after refuelling but he had not been allowed to. This time he didn't intend to be left behind, or to fail. He intended to lead the way into the Sea of Marmara.

As they sailed on, hour after hour, in the same formation, *Adamant* leading, E 14, E 15 and E 11 astern of her, the weather remained fine and Nasmith's spirits rose. There was a light easterly breeze and the wide expanse of blue sea sparkled in the sunlight under the paler blue of the sky. Small fleecy clouds lay all around the horizon, pierced far to the northward by the beautiful snow-capped peaks of the Sierra Nevada mountains. The men came up by twos and threes on to the bridge for a smoke, and to get away from the heat below and the clatter of the engines. Jupp was easing the boat along with the least possible expenditure of fuel – if they continued as they were going, if the weather bore up, they would be all right.

At night they sighted numbers of ships, brilliantly lighted and none of them in convoy, for there had so far been no sign of U Boat activity in the Mediterranean. On the evening of the fourth they saw the bright lights of the city of Algiers shining across the calm water – it was hard to believe that there was a war on.

By the morning of the sixth the weather had deteriorated. There was a fresh northerly wind. The dark blue sea was flecked with foam and E 11 was rolling and sending showers of spray over the conning tower. Nasmith had to increase the revolutions to keep up with the rest but, unless it grew worse, he was confident that he would make port with the fuel remaining. Just before dark, he sighted the distant cliffs of Malta. When the convoy reached the entrance to Grand Harbour it was after midnight; E 11's fuel was almost exhausted. The authorities at Valetta refused to open the gates in the boom defences to let them in – they didn't share the general complacency about the danger of U Boats. Not wishing to let E 11 drift away to be towed back ignominiously next day by a salvage tug, Nasmith took her into the small inlet of Marsa Scala, a mile or two farther along the coast, and sheltered there for the night.

At daylight on the morning of the 7th April, a line of buoys in the centre of the boom moved aside, and the way was clear. A fishing boat came out, felucca rigged, her white sails spread, as light as a bird. The ramparts of St. Elmo, of weather-beaten cream-coloured limestone, towered over them as they slipped through the boom: to Nasmith they seemed as grim as the walls of a prison. He was afraid he would be detained there, for more engine defects had been reported during the night, including a short-circuit in the armature of the port motor; and the star clutch was stiffer than before, requiring the united efforts of two engine-room artificers to move it. The men, in long white sweaters and dark-blue trousers, were lined up on the superstructure before and abaft the conning tower at stations for entering harbour. The boatswain's pipe called them to attention, and Nasmith saluted as they approached the larger fortress of St. Angelo, and a bugle replied from high up on the ramparts. They threaded their way among a swarm of harbour service craft, naval pinnaces with shining brass funnels, gaily-painted *dghaisas,* the Maltese gondolas, and passed several cruisers and destroyers, saluting those whose captains were senior to Nasmith. In the largest dry dock he could see the superstructure of the battle cruiser *Inflexible,* being repaired after the mine damage she had received during the attack on the Dardanelles forts.

They made fast alongside *H.M.S. Egmont,* lying below the walls of St. Angelo: she was an old wooden man o' war converted into a submarine depot ship. She looked very smart. Her sides, pierced by rows of square gun-ports, were painted black and white in horizontal stripes and her decks were covered by gleaming awnings. A long pontoon outside her served as a convenient landing-stage for the submarines.

Nasmith went at once to see Commander Somerville, the captain of *Adamant,* who was in command of the flotilla. He was an experienced submarine officer, small, wiry and energetic. In response to urgent signals, engineer officers from the Base quickly came aboard E 11. They soon decided, as Nasmith had feared, that a new armature was required for the port motor, and therefore it would be impossible for her to sail with the others on the following day; it would take at least a fortnight to replace it. Extensive tests were carried out on the clutch also, and it was discovered that the starboard intermediate shaft was fractured. The fracture was visible now as a fine irregular spiral line, as thin

22

as a hair, running along the shaft, and there was a slight whip as it revolved which accounted for the difficulty they had experienced in moving the clutch. There was no spare shaft of the right size available: a new casting would have to be sent out from Portsmouth to be milled and fitted in the Naval Dockyard in Malta. There was nothing for it but to billet the crew ashore and hand E 11 over to the dockyard maties.

Nasmith was not in a very enviable frame of mind when he joined his colleagues in *Adamant* that evening. Boyle, the captain of E 14, though senior to him was about his own age. He was lanky, loose-jointed and always carefully dressed, courteous though distant and elusive with strangers, but very ready to sympathise with Nasmith in his troubles. T. S. Brodie, captain of E 15, the newest boat in the service, was very fair and had a large head and bent shoulders. His manner with Nasmith was shy, almost self-deprecating. He had come late to submarines after some years in destroyers. He had a weary, slightly cynical expression and spoke little. His fellow officers, irreverently and quite unjustly, called him "Dummy Head", to distinguish him from his twin brother, "War Head" Brodie, also a submariner who was on the staff of Commodore Keyes at Mudros. When a number of other officers came in, and the party warmed up a little, he came out of his shell, and challenged all-comers to any known form of sport from billiards to all-in wrestling. Nasmith, however, turned in early. He used to enjoy a cigar and a glass of beer, but he had stopped both smoking and drinking, which made him rather an odd figure at times in a ship's wardroom.

Next morning, concealing his bitter disappointment, he stood with D'Oyly-Hughes on the landing-stage and watched *Adamant* sail with E 14 and E 15. He had tried to change the familiar pattern of events by continually increasing his own efficiency and that of his crew but now, in spite of all his efforts, he had again been left behind. Boyle and Brodie would precede him into the Marmara as Horton and Laurence had into the Baltic.

Another officer joined them who viewed the departure of E 14 and E 15 with similar feelings. This was Lieutenant H. G. Stoker, captain of the Australian E class submarine, AE 2, a handsome cheerful Irishman, liked by everyone, whose boat was in dry dock for repairs. When the others had passed out of sight, the two frustrated captains went over to E 11 where Nasmith had promised to show Stoker the extra fittings that the VIIIth flotilla, working out of Harwich, had found necessary to negotiate anti-submarine nets and minefields. These consisted of a sharp cutter on the bow and a jumping wire running the whole length of the boat from the bow to the top of the periscope standard, and on to the stern: there were also specially designed guards over the propellers, hydroplanes, bowcaps, and all other projections which might foul an obstruction. Stoker had brought AE 2 direct from Australia, with a crew half of Australian and half of R.N. ratings, and had not seen these modifications before.

It was only natural, of course, that Stoker had also set his heart on getting through to Constantinople. He had been with the fleet which was watching the entrance to the Dardanelles to prevent a sortie by the Turkish Fleet reinforced by the German battle cruiser *Goeben* and the light cruiser *Breslau*. These two ships, at sea when war was declared, had taken refuge in the Dardanelles and their presence there had greatly influenced Turkey to come in to the war on the side of Germany. Shortly after his arrival, he told Nasmith, preparations started for an attack on the Dardanelles defences, and he formed the opinion that an attempt to dive a submarine through the Straits into the Sea of Marmara would succeed. He wrote to the Admiral saying that he was quite certain the feat could be performed if one exercised the greatest possible care in navigation. With this letter lying on the wardroom table he ran AE 2 straight on to the rocks at Sangrada Point at the entrance to Mudros Harbour: a navigation light had been extinguished to deceive the enemy! This unfortunate accident resulted in "a distinct loss of popularity with the Admiral," and the indefinite postponement of the attempt. Now, like Nasmith, he was moving heaven and earth to get his repairs completed quickly. In the meantime there was nothing that either of them could do.

Nasmith got away first. He did it by arranging for the rough casting of his shaft to be sent direct to Mudros to be fitted there by the repair ship *Reliance*. Thus he was able to sail as soon as his armature was ready. The morning of the 15th, when they left Malta, was clear and sparkling. He kept well to the south of Sicily, but he saw the dim form of Mount Etna in the distance with a motionless inverted cone of dark smoke above it. On the sixteenth the weather had changed; there was a grey sky, and long grey seas, more like Atlantic than Mediterranean weather, but in spite of the uneasy motion of the boat, the shaft held. Their next landfall was the southern coast of Greece, the tops of the mountains being visible twenty miles away, and then their mist-enshrouded slopes.

At dawn on the 18th they were off the island of Lemnos, its

hills rose-coloured in the morning light. As they approached they could see smoke rising from many ships that were hidden from view in Mudros Harbour. At 7 a.m., exchanging recognition signals with a patrolling French destroyer, they turned towards the entrance, following the route that had been given to them to avoid the anti-submarine nets being laid by drifters. A number of French transports lay in the outer roadstead. They rounded Sangrada Point, where Stoker had run ashore in AE 2, and came in sight of the huge inner harbour so crowded with ships that there didn't appear to be room for any more. It was like a great naval review. They counted a dozen battleships with cruisers, destroyers, transports crowded with troops, hospital ships and supply ships in attendance, and swarms of smaller craft, tugs, pinnaces, lighters and Greek sailing vessels. They passed along the lines of ships, past the Russian cruiser *Askold* with its five tall funnels close together, the French flagship *Suffren*, the great battleship *Queen Elizabeth*, pride of the fleet, the balloon-carrying ship *Manica*, and at 7.30 a.m. made fast alongside *Adamant*. The harbour was surrounded by a flat plain, bare of vegetation except low scrub, and the ground rose in a gentle slope to a line of arid hills with rounded contours. The plain and the lower slopes of the hills were covered with the white tents of military encampments. Clouds of dust rose among them, stirred up by the feet of marching columns. There was a miserable village with a church and a wooden pier, but little further sign of normal occupation except for a few scattered farm buildings. Dead horses and mules floated among the ships in the harbour, the legs of some of them sticking up like periscopes.

As soon as Nasmith boarded *Adamant* he sensed that something was wrong. Somerville met him on the quarter-deck and conducted him at once to his cabin. There he told him that T. S. Brodie in E 15 had started for the Marmara on the night of the 16th, but had run aground near Kephez and been shot up by the shore batteries. "He was in a great hurry," Somerville said, "to get going before you arrived. There was a rumour that you were coming a couple of days earlier. He had his E.R.A.s, and my engineers, working all night before he sailed, on a defective hydroplane."

"Were there – casualties?" Nasmith asked.

"We don't know yet. Brodie's brother spotted her aground yesterday. He had followed her up in a seaplane." Somerville showed him the position on the chart. E 15 lay only a few hundred yards from Fort 8, and the problem was how to prevent the Turks getting her off and using her against the Allies. McArthur had tried to torpedo her in B 6, but missed. During the night, two destroyers, *Scorpion* and *Grampus,* had gone in, but failed to find her. Now B 11 was trying to reach her.

Nasmith suggested taking E 11 up to torpedo the stranded submarine, and going on into the Marmara, but Somerville wouldn't hear of it. He said that if the fractured shaft should break there could be a serious accident. It would be better for Nasmith to get his repairs done, and be ready when his turn came. Nasmith had to admit that it was unlikely any senior officer would take the responsibility of letting him start out with an engine defect. The appropriate signals were made, and that same afternoon they went in *Adamant's* boat to the repair ship *Reliance,* an ex-liner converted into a floating workshop. They were welcomed cordially by the commanding officer, Engineer Captain Humphries. His staff were working on the top priority job of converting the old collier, *River Clyde,* into a landing ship, but it was arranged that the *Reliance* engineers should lift out E 11's shaft and flywheel – which entailed first removing her after superstructure and the plates of her hull above the engine-room – and supervise the fitting of the new shaft, but that E 11's artificers and stokers should turn the rough casting on the lathe and fit the clutch. It was estimated that, working day and night shifts, the job would take three weeks.

TWO

Nasmith never doubted that he would be going up to the Marmara as soon as E 11 was ready, and he intended to collect every scrap of information that might help him to succeed. On leaving *Reliance* he continued up the harbour to the converted merchantman *Hindu Kush,* parent ship of the five B class and three French submarines operating from Mudros. They were being used to watch the enemy ports from which the British supply routes might be attacked, particularly Smyrna, and to lie in wait in case the *Goeben* and *Breslau* should make a sortie from the Dardanelles. Here Lieutenant-Commander Pownall was in command, another submariner, an old and close friend. He had little information except the report of Lieutenant-Commander Holbrook's exploit in the previous December. Holbrook had won the first naval V.C. of the war by taking B 11 twelve miles up the Straits to Sari Siglar Bay, and torpedoing and sinking the old Turkish battleship *Messoudieh* although she was protected by four lines of mines. B 11 had been chosen because she had new batteries, but she had returned with them exhausted after contending with fierce currents, particularly off the European shore. Shortly after this, the French submarine *Saphir* had tried to get through and had been lost at Nagara Point due, it was thought, to the strong currents. B 11 had not come across any anti-submarine nets, Pownall said, but in March a trawler had fouled a line of buoys supporting a net off the Suandere River. With the assistance of a destroyer she had attempted to tow it away, but had been driven off by the shore batteries.

"We're not the first," Pownall said, "to try conclusions with the Dardanelles – or the 'Hellespont,' as the ancients called it. The Greeks, in their expedition against Troy, had to sacrifice a princess before they could get a wind strong enough to sail their ships against the current; then there was Xerxes in 448 B.C., King of the Persians. To invade Greece he had to get his army across the Hellespont. He built a bridge of boats, but the current swept it away; so he punished it with three hundred lashes, and cursed it, calling it 'a salt and treacherous stream.' That was curious because it's fresh water, but I suppose he would find it rather brackish if he tried to drink it."

He suggested that Nasmith should see Lieutenant-Commander Brodie, brother of the missing captain of E 15, who as personal assistant to Roger Keyes would know most about the problem.

Holbrook failed that afternoon to reach and destroy E 15 owing to a heavy mist in the Straits. Aeroplanes bombed her without effect, and the battleships *Triumph* and *Majestic* fired on her at long range without scoring a hit. Finally two naval picket boats under the leadership of Commander E. Robinson made a daring attack during the night of the 18th-19th and in spite of heavy gunfire and dazzling searchlights, succeeded in torpedoing her. One of the picket boats was sunk, but the crew were taken aboard the other.

On the 20th, Nasmith went over to the *Queen Elizabeth* to see Brodie, taking D'Oyly and Brown. A strong breeze had sprung up, and consequently the preliminary movements of the invasion fleet, timed for the 21st, had been cancelled.

Brodie met them on the quarter-deck as Nasmith was piped over the side. It was a shock to see his uncanny resemblance to

27

his twin brother. He conducted them to his cabin and, as soon as they were settled, he tried to put them at their ease:

"I have noticed," he began, "in some of my colleagues a reluctance to talk about E 15, to spare my feelings, but it is absolutely necessary that we should analyse the causes of the disaster. I want you to know that you can do so with complete freedom. It is not painful to me now to talk about my brother – quite the contrary."

"You have news of him?" Nasmith asked eagerly.

"Yes. This morning Roger Keyes brought me this. . . ." He fumbled in his notebook and brought out a printed "Intelligence" slip. "It was typical of him to bring it me himself, wasn't it? It is a translation of a paragraph in a Turkish newspaper about E 15." In a firm voice he read a line here and there, " '. . . the captain and three of his crew were killed outright by a direct hit on the conning tower . . . they were buried on the beach with military honours . . . the captain had a very white skin. . . .' " He folded the slip and put it away in his pocket. The other officers murmured their sympathy. He thanked them quietly, and continued, "At first I couldn't take it in, I had felt quite sure that he was all right. And then I saw that my intuition had been a true one – he was all right but not in the way I had imagined.

"Shortly before your arrival from Malta – on the 14th, Keyes summoned a conference, here in the Q.E. He had previously told me to collect all available information about the Straits. I'm afraid there was little I could tell them. Our Intelligence supplied us with a wonderful map – here it is." He unrolled a map. ". . . with the mines all neatly marked in red, you see, and the shore batteries, torpedo tubes, searchlights. The only item of value came from French sources . . ." He opened a folder. ". . . a sketch map of the Straits, emanating from Krupps, together with the specifications of a submarine. It seems that the Germans, while the Greeks were at war with the Turks, had been trying to sell them one of their U Boats which, they claimed, would be able to reach as far as Nagara, where the Turkish heavy ships usually lay. You'd better take this, Nasmith, and study it." He pushed the folder across the table. "You'll see that they claimed a battery endurance of 13 hours at a diving speed of $4\frac{1}{2}$ knots, giving a range of about 60 miles submerged.

"That was all that I had to offer the conference, except for one rather legendary story . . . It seems that a redundant member of the Sultan's household was dropped into the Marmara in the customary weighted sack, and when they imagined that it was

28

well on its way to the Mediterranean, it turned up again under the walls of the Seraglio. . . . Interesting?

"Of course, the Krupps memo was the most important. We were all trying to estimate the amount of endurance of an E boat's battery against a current of x strength at 90 feet, when Keyes, to whom algebra makes no appeal, cut us short with an abrupt question, 'Do you think an E boat can make it?' He was looking at Somerville.

"We had all expected to discuss how it was to be done, not if it was possible. Somerville straightened up and deliberated a second or two. Obviously his answer carried a big responsibility. Then he firmly said 'No.' Pownall, who had a more academic interest and probably a more judicial mind than the rest of us, said 'No,' equally decisively. Keyes looked at me. Knowing even more surely than the others how he would hate my answer, and feeling that I had somehow betrayed him, my 'No' came next. It had to be my answer, but I was meanly thankful I had not had to give it first. Boyle's 'No' was certainly the result of his own judgment. There remained only my brother: his shy but confident 'Yes' was electrifying. Keyes jumped to his feet and said, 'Well, it's got to be tried, and you shall do it.' It was rather hard on Boyle. The question was not if they were prepared to go – naturally they were both prepared to go – but whether they considered it possible.

"Two days later E 15 sailed. I went with them as far as Tenedos and spent the night on the stone floor of a Greek farmhouse there, striving hard to believe that the venture was not a hopeless one.

"As soon as it was light enough, I went off in a seaplane to look for E 15. It was a fresh cloudless morning and the view was arrestingly beautiful. When we crossed the white sandy beach under Kephez Point I saw a slim grey straw at right angles to the line of the shore, and a smaller black straw at an acute angle beside it: I knew them for E 15 with thin oily smoke coming up from her conning tower, and a Turkish torpedo boat already investigating. I realised it was failure, and, for E 15, final."

There was silence for a few moments. Brodie got up and looked out of the porthole at the great fleet waiting for the signal to weigh anchor, and at the storm clouds drifting above it. Then he turned to Nasmith again, "We don't know what happened. He and I plotted his course together, and apparently we didn't make sufficient allowance for the underwater eddies. The Admiralty charts, as you know, give only the surface currents. The problem is to find out what goes on down below. I wish I could be more helpful. Have you any questions?"

"Surely it would have been quite easy," Nasmith said, "to measure the underwater currents in peacetime?"

"Neither we, nor the Turks, apparently, ever thought of doing so," he replied. "At least there are no records."

"We had a Naval Mission in Constantinople," Nasmith went on, "training the Turkish Navy, right up till the outbreak of hostilities. Can't Admiral Limpus or his staff tell us anything?"

"There's been a high-level decision about that," Brodie said. "Admiral Limpus and his staff have been instructed not to supply any information which could be used against the Turks."

"Why not?"

"Well . . . I suppose it wouldn't be considered quite – gentlemanly. He should, in fact, be in command now instead of De Robeck but he as been sent to Malta, to be well out of the way."

The E 11 officers looked at each other rather grimly. After a pause, Nasmith said it would be helpful if Brodie would describe his experiences while co-ordinating the efforts to destroy E 15.

"Yes, I would like to do that," Brodie said, "for several things happened which might be important for you to know about if you are to avoid our mistakes. On the night of the 18th I went up with the destroyers – I was in Scorpion, commanded by A. B. Cunningham. As we crept up the Asiatic coast at half speed on the eastern edge of the searchlight's arc, our progress seemed interminably slow; to port there was a smooth brilliantly lit expanse of sea, to starboard featureless blackness hiding the shore, uncomfortably close. At last we were blindingly in the full glare somewhere abreast of Kephez. A fixed light, trained downwards, completely hid E 15 and the shore. We knew we must have been seen, but nothing happened. 'They won't fire till we turn,' said Cunningham as he rang down 'Full ahead,' ordered 'Hard astarboard,' and opened fire on the searchlight. 'We shan't hit it, but it keeps the men happy.' The guns of the fort opened up on us as we swung, and a number of light field guns as well – we were lucky to get out of it.

"At dawn I went up again, this time in submarine B 6. We sighted E 15 about a mile away, and then a curious thing happened: as we approached submerged and thinking we were still some distance from her, we heard the unmistakable s-s-s of a keel on sand as we drove gently up the beach. We had fallen into the same trap – we were ashore beside her. There must be a deep current setting in very strongly towards Kephez. 'Hard astarboard! Speed up!' McArthur ordered, for there was deep water to port. The depth-gauge had risen to nothing, the periscope was looking at the sky. We all knew that the conning tower and the whole forward superstructure were above water. I clambered up and looked out of the starboard scuttle: on our beam, less than a hundred yards away, was E 15, heeled right over, nearly bottom up. I could see the underside of her port saddle tank, like a huge pink blister on her grey-green hull. The picket boats had done their job. She was a complete wreck.

"My first feeling of triumph that the Turks had not got E 15 was succeeded by fear that they had got B 6. The muzzles of the guns in the shore battery looked horribly close. The thought of the Brodie twins losing two submarines by identical blunders filled me with rage. Meanwhile McArthur had ordered 'Blow 1 and 2' – the main ballast – and called to the helmsman to report her head. Slowly she swung round and slid off into deep water."

Nasmith, who had been listening with intense concentration in order not to miss a detail that could be of importance in forming his own plans, suddenly asked, "At what depth did you approach Kephez?"

"We never went below forty feet."

"Forty feet? What about the minefield? Shouldn't you have been at least at sixty or seventy?"

"Indeed we should. But you know these old B class boats with no bow planes ... It took the coxswain plenty of juggling with the diving rudders even to keep her at that."

As Nasmith seemed lost in thought, D'Oyly asked, "What about the guns? Didn't they open up on you lying on the beach with your conning tower sticking out of the water?"

"No, they didn't – they must have been having a stand easy. But they opened up all right while we were sliding down into the depths. We could hear the bursts hammering against the hull fortunately getting fainter and fainter as we retreated."

"You slid – how far down into the depths?" It was Nasmith again.

"As we slid off the shelf of sand, the bows dipped steeply, and suddenly we were diving down at a quite unmanageable angle. My feet slipped from under me: I clung on desperately with my hands, expecting quick disaster. The depth-gauge raced from seventeen to eighty feet while the coxswain was sweating at his diving rudders, and McArthur reversed his trimming orders. Before I dreamed that this could take effect, she levelled off. I stood up, and found to my amazement that she had steadied at ninety feet. We were slowing down and under easy control."

"Extraordinary. . . ." Nasmith clasped his hands in front of him in excitement. "You had no further trouble?"

"None at all."

"Indeed I'm most grateful," he said. "At last we have something to go on. I suppose you followed the course you helped to plot for E 15?"

"Yes – a few degrees to eastward of it."

"Well . . . I wonder if we could check up on some of the leading marks, positions of guns and searchlights, and so on? Have you got those charts, Brown?" . . . and for the next hour or so they were engrossed in technical details.

On the 21st of April AE 2 arrived at Mudros. Stoker, on the eve of sailing from Malta, had heard of the loss of E 15 but his enthusiasm was undaunted. Nasmith was fairly confident that the embargo on risking further submarines in the Straits would last until E 11 was ready, but on the 23rd a signal was received ordering Stoker to report at once on board the flagship. Keyes told him briefly that if he still believed it possible to dive through the Dardanelles, he would be permitted to try. He took him to Admiral De Robeck who found it hard to believe that the difficulties could be overcome, but said he had decided the military value would be so great that it must be tried again. If he got through, the other boats would immediately be sent to follow. "If you succeed," he concluded, "there is no calculating the result it will cause, and it may well be that you will have done more to finish the war than any other act accomplished."

After a month of almost constant bad weather, the wind had moderated and ships all over Mudros Harbour were preparing for sea. The first to leave were three transports carrying the battalions forming the advance parties to be landed at Cape Helles and Morto Bay. They were followed by the cruiser *Euryalus,* flying the flag of Rear-Admiral Wemyss, the battle cruiser *Implacable* and the battleship *Cornwallis.* The troops in the other ships were cheering them as they passed. The next to sail was the *River Clyde,* and then one after another the ships hove up their anchors and left in an orderly procession which continued without interruption for the next three days and nights until the great harbour was nearly denuded of shipping. *Queen Elizabeth,* flying the flag of Vice-Admiral De Robeck, and carrying General Sir Ian Hamilton and his staff, sailed on the afternoon of the 24th.

It seemed that Stoker had scarcely left when he was back with a broken shaft controlling the forward hydroplanes. In a few hours, repairs had been effected and permission gained from the Admiral for another attempt. This time it would coincide with the troop landings, so Keyes amended his orders. Instead of endeavouring to get up to the Marmara unobserved, he was to attack enemy vessels reported to be dropping mines in the Narrows off Chanak: it was a measure to protect the battleships and troop transports operating at the mouth of the Dardanelles.

At 3 a.m. on Sunday April 25th, AE 2 again entered the Dardanelles, and as she slipped along in the darkness and in the fitful glare of the searchlights, nearly 200 ships astern of her were approaching the inhospitable coast. At 5.15 a.m. the peace of the morning was shattered by the roar of guns, as the whole fleet opened fire on the coastline to cover the landings, and continued until the small boats towed by steam pinnaces were close to the beaches. The landings were furiously opposed by machine-gun and rifle fire, but at all except two points the invading forces were able to get ashore and establish themselves. The most serious check was opposite the main Turkish position at Cape Helles where the beach is dominated by buildings and rising ground. That part of the invading force attempting to land from open boats was practically wiped out, and so were the first troops to land from the *River Clyde* which had been run ashore near the ancient fortress of Seddul Bahr. Pownall, who had volunteered as Beach Master, was killed in the leading boat. In spite of the violent bombardment, no progress could be made until nightfall when the remainder of the troops landed and stormed the cliffs. French troops, after a successful holding attack on Kum Kale, on the Asiatic side, were withdrawn and landed at Helles. No message had been received from AE 2. Enemy wireless reports spoke of frustrated landings and a British submarine ashore off Chanak.

Just after midnight, Admiral Thursby came aboard *Queen Elizabeth* accompanied by two brigadier-generals of the Anzac Corps bringing a letter from General Birdwood containing an alarming report of the exhaustion of the men under him. It suggested that an immediate re-embarkation might be necessary. Sir Ian Hamilton was aroused, and a conference summoned in the fore cabin. While he was penning his reply, Brodie intruded and, ignoring furious gestures of dismissal from Keyes, insisted on him reading a signal which the yeoman had just handed him. It was from AE 2, reporting that she had got through the

Narrows and had torpedoed a Turkish gunboat. The conference instantly realised its significance, and General Birdwood was able to encourage his men with the news that an Australian submarine was across the Turks main supply route. The Australians had already re-established their positions, but the heartening effect of Stoker's success on all the front-line troops was real enough, By the morning of the 26th what many had thought impossible had been achieved – the successful invasion of a heavily fortified enemy coastline.

Within a few hours of the receipt of Stoker's signal, Lieutenant-Commander Boyle in his turn was received on board the flagship. He was briefed by Keyes who, as Brodie expressed it, communicated his enthusiasm rather than any definite orders or information. At 3 a.m. on the 27th, E 14 entered the Straits, her destroyer escort turned back and she went on alone into the ghostly glare of the searchlights. At 4 a.m. the sound of heavy firing was heard from the Turkish battery at Suandere – then there was silence. Twenty-four hours later she signalled that she was in the Marmara.

While rejoicing in the success of his colleagues, Nasmith was naturally disappointed that he had had no part in the breakthrough to the Marmara about which he had thought and planned for so long. The history of the break-through to the Baltic had exactly repeated itself – two captains had got through, and he, who by common consent should have been the leader, had been left behind: but he was relieved to know that the difficulties which to him had seemed so formidable had apparently been easily overcome by the others. The situation, however, changed overnight, and it became abundantly clear that there was still a job for Nasmith to do as soon as the repairs on E 11 could be completed. The French submarine *Joule,* commanded by Lieutenant de Vaisseau du Petit-Thouars, whose eagerness greatly impressed the British Admiral, was now ready, and on the 30th April she entered the Straits. A few hours later, the enemy announced that she had been sunk with all hands, a message impossible to doubt as the compressed air storage chamber of one of her torpedoes was picked up at the entrance to the Dardanelles that afternoon. This was not the end of the bad news. The same night a signal in English from the German cruiser *Breslau* informed Admiral De Robeck that AE 2 had been sunk by a Turkish gunboat, but the crew had all been picked up. So the two captains who had believed the venture possible met with disaster, and only Boyle, who had believed it impossible, survived.

Meanwhile E 11 lay in Mudros Harbour alongside *Reliance,* the after end of her superstructure open to the sky and her engines dismantled. While the crew were exercised ashore, Nasmith went in a launch to the island of Tenedos where he landed at a small harbour crowded with mine-sweeping trawlers under an old castle. He was met by Commander Samson of the Royal Naval Air Service who commanded the seaplane base on the island which consisted of a commandeered farm, a large white ensign and an improvised airstrip. A two-seater Farman biplane was provided for a flight up the Straits. When Nasmith had climbed into the observer's seat, the pilot, Lieutenant Bell-Davis, passed him a machine gun in case they should meet a German fighter. He fired a few rounds to see how it worked, as he had never used one before, and they took off.

A few minutes later they were over the Narrows and Nasmith was looking down anxiously to see if he could spot a line of buoys that would indicate the presence of a net, or any large ship which he might torpedo on the way up. The two battleships *Barbarossa* and *Turgut Reiss* had been lying between Kilid Bahr and Nagara Point bombarding the beaches, but they had withdrawn and there was no sign of them. Some enemy guns opened up, but the brown shrapnel bursts were well below them. He had hoped to see the mines and establish their exact location, but the sun glittering on the rippling water made it impossible to see anything beneath the surface. There was apparently no net in position, but the lighthouses were clearly visible, which was of the greatest importance to him as he would have to identify them later in brief glimpses through his periscope. Finally he had one of the greatest thrills of his life – his first sight of the Marmara, serene and shining in the evening light. And he realised also what a very small part of the Peninsula was so far in British hands.

On the 10th May the new shaft was ready, but it took another two days to lower it into the boat again and get it level. Then the plates of the pressure hull were securely riveted, the after superstructure was replaced, and E 11 was ready for sea.

While still alongside *Reliance,* the engines were started and the routine of "In clutch" – "Out clutch" was repeated again and again until Nasmith was satisfied that it moved freely. They cast off and made for the harbour entrance. The boat was fairly ship-shape, though not yet scrubbed and polished as she would be in the ensuing days, and for the first time in many weeks Nasmith listened happily to the sweet sound of two smoothly running engines. A snatch of song came up the open conning tower hatch, and a burst of laughter. Somerville was on board for the trials with engineers and fitters from *Reliance*: they were with D'Oyly in the engine-room who glowered suspiciously and critically examined every fitting that had been removed and replaced during the repairs as if they couldn't possibly have put it back exactly as it should have been.

When they reached the open sea, the canvas screen round the bridge was taken down, and the stanchions supporting it were unshipped and stowed away; the coxswain was relieved at the wheel by a seaman and went below. They tested the shaft at gradually increasing speeds up to the maximum revolutions. "She's running sweetly," Jupp reported, "better than the old one!"

Brown, with a chart spread out on the wardroom table, reported that they were nearing the area appointed for their diving tests – for they needed practice dives to adjust the trim and to test the new rivets in the pressure hull. Nasmith glanced around – there were several ships on the misty-blue horizon, but none very near except their escorting trawler stationed to give warning of their presence. He called to the messenger, who was in the control room immediately below the open hatch, to inform Commander Somerville that he proposed to dive in ten minutes, and also dictated a signal to the trawler. Then he asked Brown, "What water is there?"

"Ninety fathoms, sir."

Plowman reported, "Message passed, sir."

Nasmith rang down "Slow" on the telegraph, and then "Stop." As she lost way he sent the helmsman below – he closed the lid of the magnetic compass and screwed it down, then disappeared through the conning tower hatch and continued steering before another compass in the control room. Brown collected the binoculars and the gyro compass repeater, trailing on a long lead, and followed. Nasmith nodded to the signalman and the look-out to go below also. He remained alone on the bridge for a few moments, looking at his watch, then he bent down and pressed a button just inside the connng tower hatch coaming. Immediately warning Klaxons, with a raucous sound quite unlike all the other sounds in the boat, blared through the interior from horns forward and aft.

"Diving stations!'

The men went quickly each to his appointed place and waited while D'Oyly checked personally that all the hatches were properly secured, and that the men detailed for the job had closed the ventilators which admitted the air necessary for the surface engines, but when submerged would admit water. If seawater got to the rows of four-foot high batteries under the boards of the alleyway, chlorine gas would be formed which would choke the crew to death in a matter of minutes. He reported, "Shut off for diving, sir!" Jupp reported, "Both engine clutches out!"

Nasmith stepped into the conning tower hatch, closing the lid after him, and securing it, and climbed down the steel ladder into the electrically lit interior. A seaman closed the lower hatch.

"Slow ahead on the motors," he ordered. The telegraph rang. A quiet humming sound like a swarm of bees filled the boat as the motors started and drove her slowly forward. "Flood 1,2,5, 6,7 and 8.'

D'Oyly repeated then implemented the orders, "Open 1,2,5, 6,7 and 8 Kingstons and main vents!" Stokers repeated the orders back to D'Oyly as they pulled the levers that opened the giant Kingston valves admitting seawater that hissed and gurgled into the main ballast tanks. At the same time two seamen screwed open the vent valves above their heads, and air hissed from the manifolds. The boat began to settle down in the water; the long needles of the depth-gauges stirred and wavered, registering six feet, and stopped.

"How's the bubble?" Nasmith asked.

"Three degrees by the stern, sir."

"Flood the auxiliary. Flood 3 and 4." The depth-gauge needles moved again. "How is she?"

"Horizontal. Ten feet, sir."

"Close the main vents. Take her down. Twenty feet."

The two coxwains spun their brass wheels, one operating the forward and the other the after hydroplanes – the horizontal diving rudders. The boat sank lower till the depth-gauge needles touched twenty feet. The top of the conning tower was now just below the surface, and the buoyancy was sufficiently reduced for the coxwains to control the depth as she moved forward.

"Up periscope." Wheeler pressed an electric switch: the larger of the two periscopes rose and pushed its hooded lens out of the water. Grasping the training handles, Nasmith bent down to the rubber-padded eye-piece, and walked round, turning it with him, and methodically examined the surface of the sea above them, sector by sector, noting particularly that the trawler was standing clear.

"Down periscope." Wheeler touched the switch, and the periscope slid down again, the lower end disappearing into a well in the deck.

D'Oyly came into the control room and reported that no leaks were apparent so far.

Nasmith turned to the coxswain, "Take her down to fifty feet." The coxswain and second coxswain, sitting on low stools in front of the depth-gauge, spun their big brass wheels again. A very slight incline forward became noticeable. The depth-gauge needles crept slowly round the dials – forty – forty-five – forty-eight.... "Keep her up, Coxswain," Nasmith said sharply. She dipped to fifty-five, then came back to fifty and steadied. "Fifty feet, sir."

The hydroplane indicators showed by the amount of 'rise' they were now carrying, that the boat was slightly heavy forward, so they pumped water into the after interior compensating tank until the coxswains could keep her level, with the hydroplanes amidships.

D'Oyly again searched for leaks round the new rivets, with a piece of chalk in his hand ready to mark them, but he couldn't find any. They went down to a hundred and twenty feet – the limit marked on the gauges – but still there were no leaks. She was as sound as a drum, and D'Oyly and Nasmith were satisfied that she was seaworthy. They returned to Mudros, went alongside *Adamant* and filled up with stores and fresh water. The following day, they sailed for Imbros.

THREE

Meanwhile the military situation was unchanged. The Allied Troops were firmly established on the tip of the Gallipoli Peninsula, and the Turks were unable to dislodge them. They had attacked the Allied lines furiously for three days without success on the first, second and third of May – an action known as the Battle of Krithia – and the Allied counter-attacks on the sixth, seventh and eighth had been equally unsuccessful. The landings, in spite of heavy losses, had succeeded beyond expectation, but subsequent progress had been disappointing. The peak of Achi

Baba dominating the scene remained unconquered. At first the ships of the fleet had provided powerful artillery support, but the enemy was learning not to expose his troops to their fire, and he had driven his lines so close up to our own that it was impossible to bombard the one without causing casualties in the other. Shortages of ammunition were already being felt on both sides.

In a daring sortie on the night of the 9th May, a Turkish torpedo boat had sunk the British battleship *Goliath* with serious loss of life off the entrance to the Dardanelles. On the 14th *Queen Elizabeth* was withdrawn and left Imbros for England. Admiral De Robeck transferred his flag to *Lord Nelson*. Sir Ian Hamilton had already removed with his staff to the *S.S. Arcadian.*

When it was reported to Keyes that E 11 was ready, he gave instructions that the next time W/T contact was made with E 14, she should be ordered to return. Nasmith was ordered to await her arrival. He used the time to exercise his crew in practice dives, reproducing as nearly as possible the conditions they might be called upon to face.

The first problem would be the long dive up the Straits, so he made a long practice dive, remaining submerged and under way for twelve hours. Considering that they had no reserves of air except what happened to be in the boat when they submerged, the men stood this rather better than the batteries which were found to be practically exhausted. Next, to convince the men by a practical demonstration that the boat would not necessarily be in danger if they dived below the official safety limits, he took her down to the lowest indications marked on the depth-gauges, and went on down till D'Oyly swore that the steel plates of the hull between the frames were bulging inwards under the terrific pressure. They straightened out again as they rose and pressure was reduced, and only one small leak appeared by one of the new rivets. During these dives the men were moved about from one job to another – stokers were steering, E.R.A.s working the hydroplane wheels, seamen tending the switchboards, and so on.

Next, crash dives were rehearsed again and again, sometimes from running on the diesels, sometimes from charging on one diesel and going ahead on the other, sometimes from running on the motors though surfaced. In the latter case, with the ventilators already closed and not having to de-clutch, they could slip under so quickly that a special drill had to be worked out so that those on the bridge wouldn't be left swimming. It would normally be at night, or in poor visibility that this would apply. The boat would already be well trimmed down, with only the conning tower showing, and on the bridge there would only be Nasmith, or the officer of the watch, keeping a look-out forward, and a seaman keeping a look-out aft. The helmsman would be steering from below, and the coxswain sitting with his hand on the hydroplane wheel. If the seaman sighted a bow wave in the darkness, he had to bang Nasmith on the back and leap down the conning tower hatch, and Nasmith would follow, sounding the klaxons as he went. Whereupon the coxswain would at once take her down while D'Oyly closed the lower conning tower hatch. If Nasmith sighted a bow wave, he would bang the look-out on the back who would make a dive for the hatch, and Nasmith would follow – and if he was imprisoned between the two hatches, or left in the sea, it would just be too bad. D'Oyly had strict orders not to delay the dive to let him get down. When they had rehearsed this a dozen times, it was surprising how quickly they could do it.

Finally – the supreme test – he announced that they were going to exercise their duties in darkness. He allowed them only a few dim emergency lights from dry batteries. As they dived – some of them must have thought that it was for the last time – the brightest light was a spot of daylight reflected through the periscope which gradually died on the corner of the compressor pump as they went deeper. Nasmith had carried out this test with all his crews since a nightmare experience of his while in command, before the war, of the submarine A 4. They were experimenting with underwater sound waves on a calm day at Portsmouth. Though trimmed down, they had to signal to another vessel through an open ventilator. For some unknown reason – perhaps it was the swell caused by a distant fast-moving ship, the boat started 'bucketing.' She dipped her bows, water poured in through the ventilator, and in an instant she was heading for the bottom at an angle of 40 degrees in pitch darkness, chlorine gas pouring from the batteries, and all metal, when touched with the naked hand, giving an electric shock. Because he had trained himself to work in the dark, he was able to leap to the ventilator and thrust his arm into it to partly check the inward rush of water while he directed his men blowing all the ballast tanks. The painful pressure on his arm gradually eased and she surfaced in time for the men to be got out before they were overcome by the fumes. E 11, however, remained under perfect control. When Nasmith was satisfied that his men wouldn't make a mistake, even in the dark, he told the coxswain to bring her up, and blew the main ballast. Compressed air hissed into the tanks, the hydroplane wheels turned, and soon the spot of daylight appeared again, getting brighter and brighter until they surfaced and practice diving was over for the day. As they returned to the anchorage, recharging their batteries as they went, some of the men were wondering what they would have to practise next – perhaps bubble, bubble, bubble – and getting out and walking home along the bed of the ocean – but fortunately E 14 returned, to everyone's relief, surfacing near one of the French battleships, and a signal was received ordering Nasmith to report that evening on board the flagship.

E 11 lay all day at Kephalo alongside the destroyer *Grasshopper,* the starboard diesel engine charging the batteries. The men had been told to get as much rest as possible, so they were lounging about, reading, sleeping or writing letters – the mail would close at eight in the evening. Behind the long green curtains of the wardroom, which was between the control room and the forward torpedo room, Nasmith sat with D'Oyly and Brown, studying the charts. They had done all they could think of to prepare the crew for whatever might happen; the engines and every piece of equipment on board had been inspected and thoroughly tested – but they were aware that the captains of the lost submarines had also done all they could to prepare for emergencies. It was no ordinary hazard that had caused the loss of four out of the five sumarines that had attempted what they were about to attempt. There was no explanation for the loss of E 15, *Saphir* and *Joule*; and as for AE 2, she must have already been in trouble – or else very unlucky – to be sunk by an enemy gunboat. The only clue to the mystery had been provided by C. G. Brodie in their talk in the *Queen Elizabeth* in which he had described the strange behaviour of the submarine B 6 when she went up to investigate the loss of E 15. First she hadn't been able to get down below 40 feet, secondly she had been swept on to the beach when the captain, who had just had a look through the periscope, thought they were still some distance from it, thirdly, when she got off again, the boat had apparently fallen straight down as though falling through space – but not to the bottom. At 90 feet, as though landing on a ledge, she had suddenly straightened out and regained her trim. This was an amazing performance, and if they could account for it, they might be well on the way to explaining the loss of the other boats, and to preventing E 11 meeting a like fate. Nasmith thought of the

41

Dardanelles as a river – as indeed it had been in fact until comparatively recently, in geological time, that is – and he knew that the water in a broad swift-flowing river coming to a bend can roll right over, causing, therefore, a cross current on the surface, with an up current on one side of the bend and a down current on the other. If this was the case at Kephez, it would explain why B 6 found it difficult to submerge on one side against an up current, was swept across the stream on to the beach by the cross current and then went straight down with the down current – but why only to 90 feet? Some other factor must influence the play of the current at this depth. There was something about it he didn't understand, something he must understand if E 11 was to survive. He frowned over the course he and Brown had laid off on the chart. Five other captains of submarines had done the same, probably laying off identical courses, as they were all working from the same obviously inadequate information, and it had led four of them to destruction. All he could do was to alter his course much closer to the European side to avoid being rolled over towards Kephez as E 15 and B 6 had been.

His plan to get up the Straits, based on the Admiralty charts, called for 20 hours submerged. That was far beyond E 11's capacity. Her economical cruising speed under the surface was three knots. The charts indicated adverse currents of up to four knots round Nagara Point, and between Kilid Bahr and Chanak – it would mean increasing to seven knots in these sections, which would exhaust the batteries at a tremendous rate. It would mean also that he would have to surface somewhere on the way, and remain on the surface for some hours to recharge his batteries, but there was nowhere to lie on the surface out of range of the enemy's guns. According to the Krupp plan, if any reliance could be placed on that, the deep currents were much weaker: he might have only a current of one knot against him.

The only additional item he had gleaned from Intelligence was that the Turks were said to be dumping obstructions, including an old iron bridge, into the channel off Nagara Point. There was nothing to be gained by discussing the other hazards with his officers. They knew all about the mines that had sunk the three battleships *Bouvet*, *Ocean* and *Irresistible* during the attack on the 18th of March – but it was not really known if this was actually due to mines, as the sector had recently been swept. It could have been floating mines, or Leon mines which automatically change from one depth to another, or it could have been shore-based torpedo tubes which had been reported at

Suandere and Kephez. He considered that, for a submarine, the navigational risks were greater than the risks of mines and torpedoes, and he decided to surface as often as necessary to establish his position.

When the picket boat came, he warned D'Oyly not to overcharge the batteries and to be ready to sail as soon as he returned. Then he set off for the flagship.

In the battleship *Lord Nelson* he found Boyle in Brodie's cabin, and except that he was tired and pale, nothing in his manner showed that he had been under a strain. There was something dreamy, almost poetic in his expression as he described his experiences with his usual odd air of detachment. He was saying that he thought he had sunk two transports, one a very large one, and two gunboats; but several of his torpedoes had failed to run, and one had hit a supply ship and failed to explode. While Brodie typed his report, Nasmith questioned him eagerly about the navigation of the Straits, the strength of the currents at various depths, what leading marks had been visible through the periscope, and where had he recharged his batteries? Boyle said that he had had little difficulty with the currents on the way up, but on the way down he had been swept off his course several times, particularly into Sari Siglar Bay. He was fired at by shore batteries and patrol craft whenever he showed his periscope, but he got through to the Marmara in twelve hours after submerging off Suandere. In the Marmara he had only been surfaced for twenty minutes when he was forced to dive again by patrols; it took him the whole of that day, and the next day and the following night to recharge his exhausted batteries, having to break the charge and dive frequently. The place was swarming with destroyers and gunboats. At last he had to stop with both motors overheated – they had been running continuously for fifty hours – and the top lens of one periscope was damaged by a shell burst. On the way down he had passed close to the Turkish battleship *Turgut Reiss,* but had no torpedo left except a defective one with a broken main air pipe. He had met AE 2 and spoken for fifteen minutes to Stoker who reported that he also had defective torpedoes: he had run ashore at Chanak after torpedoing a gunboat and stuck there with his bridge and conning tower out of the water, and he had run ashore again on the opposite side of the channel. They had made a rendezvous for the next day, but AE 2 hadn't turned up: Boyle didn't know what had happened to her. About the leading marks and the positions of the searchlights he was rather vague, and Brodie working at the typewriter was surprised at the small amount of information that one submarine captain was able to pass on to the other.

They were summoned to Admiral De Robeck's cabin. They found him, a rugged dominating figure, surrounded by his guests for the evening. He greeted them cordially and offered them a glass of sherry, which Nasmith refused. Commodore Keyes was beside him, straight as a ramrod, aggressive and alert, and Sir Ian Hamilton, Commander of the Allied Forces, with General Braithwaite, his Chief of Staff, and a dozen other high-ranking officers. They were greeted also by an old friend, Admiral Wemyss, most approachable of Admirals, with twinkling monocle and genial personality. He formed the principal liaison between the army and the navy, had organised the base at Mudros, got everybody into the right ships with supplies and ammunition, and the ships to the right places.

Sir Ian's headquarters were still in *S.S. Arcadian* lying off one of the beaches and connected to the various sectors by telephone, but it was customary for the chiefs of the two services and the Allied forces to dine together to exchange views and discuss the latest developments which, as it happened, were rather favourable: the Turks had been furiously attacking the Australian sector for the whole of the previous night – that of the 18th May – and had been repulsed with heavy loss. The overall picture of the war, however, was less reassuring. It was becoming more and more urgent to pass the Dardanelles to relieve the pressure on the Russian armies, and to get supplies to them, but the slow progress of the Allies had brought about a political crisis at home. It had been provoked by Lord Fisher, the First Sea Lord, attacking Winston Churchill, the First Lord of the Admiralty, on the subject of naval reinforcements for the campaign, and the last straw had been Churchill's proposal to send out two more E class submarines: Fisher had walked out of the Admiralty and resigned as a protest – strange news to reach the leaders of the expedition on the very day of E 14's triumphant return from the Marmara. The latest rumour was that Churchill would have to resign also. The whole situation must have been causing the gravest anxiety to Sir Ian who was himself appealing for further reinforcements and whose guns were short of ammunition.

There were eighteen of them at dinner in the sparsely furnished Admiral's cabin – sparsely furnished because of an order that everything inflammable should be removed because of fire hazards in an action. After they had drunk 'the King,' the Admiral suggested that Boyle should tell them something about

44

his trip to the Marmara. Keyes was more excited than anyone else, bubbling over with delight. Wemyss was smiling across the table to Brodie, who was sitting next to Nasmith, as if to assure him that they were not forgetting that it was his brother who had led the way in E 15. ·

Boyle stood up – he looked tall and slender – and in a modest and courteous voice, began to describe how he had entered the Dardanelles at 3 a.m. on April the 27th, and one hour later he was caught by the searchlight at Suandere. The guns there opened fire, missing ahead. He dived to ninety feet, passed under the minefield and rose to twenty-two feet one mile south of Kilid Bahr. When he raised the periscope to get his bearings it was immediately fired upon heavily from the shore – it was now daylight and a glassy calm – and by numerous surface craft. At 5.15 a.m. he passed Chanak, all the forts firing at his periscope. There were a lot of small ships and steamboats patrolling, and he saw a torpedo gunboat, *Berki-Satvet* class, at which he fired at a range of 1,600 yards. He just had time to see a large column of water as high as her mast rise from her quarter, where she was presumably hit, when he had to dip again as the men in a small steamboat were leaning over trying to catch hold of the top of his periscope. . . . Here his narrative was interrupted by some rather selfconscious laughter from the guests who didn't know whether to take him seriously or not.

Keyes, to get him started again, asked him how long it took him to get up to the Marmara? Boyle said it took him nearly thirteen hours, twelve of them submerged in a continuous dive from Suandere. His batteries were practically finished when he got there, and he couldn't recharge because the destroyers and torpedo boats hunting him were constantly passing overhead.

One of the generals asked why he didn't simply stay under the water until they went away?

Boyle hesitated, and Keyes explained that the Marmara is very deep, and a submarine in deep water must keep going – but E 14 couldn't because there was no power left in her batteries. When the motors stop, the submarine either sinks to the depths and is crushed by the pressure, or bobs to the surface, risking, in this case, being sunk by the gunfire of the patrols.

"But is it deep near the shore?" the general asked.

"I wasn't near the shore," Boyle said, "and besides the air was so foul it was difficult for the men to breathe. . . ."

There were further explanations from Keyes, and some general conversation while everyone explained to everyone else the mysteries of submarine navigation. Boyle stood waiting until the Admiral silenced his guests by asking if he had sunk any ships besides the gunboat already mentioned.

"I think so," Boyle replied. "I hit several – one was very large, a transport with two funnels and three masts – I could see men and debris hurled into the air by the explosion. It got dark soon afterwards – I didn't see her actually sink but she was very much down by the stern, I think she must have. Another I last saw in a cloud of yellow smoke: she was undoubtedly on fire. Then I had to sink one of the patrols that were firing at me all the time: she was a small gunboat with a peculiarly shaped sloping stern as if she was fitted as a minelayer – similar to the *Anitab* class."

This led to some discussion about minelayers, and the persistent reports that the Turks were dropping floating mines in the Dardanelles. There were still various theories about how the three battleships had actually been sunk on March 18th. "We have information," Keyes said, "that the enemy has 18 inch torpedo tubes mounted on two barges which might be brought down and moored on either side of the channel. Do you think they were used against you? Did you observe any tracks?"

"No – there were only guns."

"I don't care about guns. Were there any torpedoes?"

"No, sir."

This was so typical of Keyes, that a flicker of amusement passed between Nasmith and Brodie.

"By the way," Keyes went on, "I passed you a message by W/T that an enemy battleship was operating in your neighbourhood. I was rather disappointed not to hear that you had attacked her."

"I was asleep," Boyle answered simply.

There was renewed laughter and conversation during which Brodie said to Nasmith, "Good for him! Keyes doesn't realise that submarine commanders ever have to sleep."

The thread of the story was now completely lost. After a few more trivial questions the Admiral thanked Boyle and he sat down. It was clear that because of Boyle's modesty in claiming no actual sinkings, except the gunboats, the full significance of his patrol was not understood. Actually he had sunk two transports. One of them, an ex-White Star liner, was carrying a battery of artillery and 6,000 Turkish troops being rushed to the front to replace the losses in the three day Battle of Krithia.

After dinner, Nasmith asked Keyes if there was any news of the *Goeben,* and he was disappointed when Keyes told him that her last appearance was on the 7th of May when she bombarded Anzac at long range. *Queen Elizabeth* got her range and she cleared out. Latest reports were that she had been taken up through the Bosphorus to the Black Sea to be used against the Russians, but the two Turkish battleships, he said, should be considered priority targets: "Their forward gun turrets have been removed and replaced by howitzers which can lob 16 inch shells over the hills on to our beaches. Sink them if you can. I'm sending E 14 to Malta for a rest and refit, so I'll want you to stay up there until she gets back. Anything else?"

"No, sir."

"Well then – go and run amuck in the Marmara!"

He took Nasmith to the Admiral who wished him luck and dismissed him.

FOUR

At 1.10 a.m. on the 19th May, E 11 cast off and moved slowly down the open harbour of Kephalo. A few minutes later *Grasshopper* followed, quickly overtaking her. Brodie, standing on the quarterdeck of the flagship, watched them threading their way past the ghostly shapes of anchored transports and men o'war until he lost them among the deceitful shadows. He listened to the throb of the engines sounding through the night and gradually fading into the distance.

On his return from the flagship, Nasmith had called the hands to prayers under the conning tower, and then given them an enthusiastic account of E 14's exploits which had a heartening effect. Now he was standing on the bridge with D'Oyly and Brown watching the moon sink into the sea and the pale stars brighten. There was a light offshore wind – too light. He would have liked a stiff breeze to whip up the surface of the Straits and make the feather of spray kicked up by his periscope less visible, but the glass was steady and the forecast promised settled weather.

They were still ten miles from the Dardanelles, but already they could see the beam of the scarchlight at Kum Kale on the southern, Asiatic, shore searching the entrance. Above the hum of their engines coming up the open conning tower hatch and the swish of the water as their sharp bows drove steadily on, making a luminous wave in the darkness, they could hear the growl of distant gunfire. Gun flashes, like fitful lightning, flickered over the land as they approached it, and blood-red shell bursts flared and vanished. As they approached, the thud and roar of heavy explosions rose above the confused rumble, and soon they could hear the crack of rifle fire and the staccato rattle of machine guns. High on the hillside a fire was burning. The light breeze died away, the myriad stars shone in the cloudless sky and the odour of death and cordite reached out to them across the still water. The powerful beam of the Kum Kale searchlight was methodically sweeping towards the northern shore and round again. Beyond it there were more searchlights on both sides of the Straits: they counted three on the southern and five on the northern side, the more distant appearing smaller and of deeper yellow. The three white cliffs of Helles at the northern side of the entrance caught a reflection of the light and loomed out of the night.

Brown bent over the compass, "Bearing's on, sir. Cape Helles thirty-five degrees, Kum Kale 128 degrees."

"Very good," Nasmith replied, and slowed down to seven knots so that their wake would be less visible from the shore. Still following *Grasshopper,* they altered to starboard to clear the towering mass of a battleship, then turned into the entrance.

At 2.45 they passed between Cape Helles and Kum Kale. "Read the log," Nasmith reminded Brown. In the absence of sure landmarks they would have to rely principally on dead reckoning.

A heavy gun fired from Kum Kale: the projectile rushed over their heads and burst with a roar in the British lines beyond Cape Helles. They passed the ruined fortress of Seddul Bahr, the "Barrier of the Sea," now in British hands, and at 3.10 reached the line of trawlers patrolling across the Straits to give warning of any sortie by enemy destroyers against the vulnerable transports and men o'war of the blockading fleet.

Four miles up they passed between two shadowy destroyers, and then a tiny light flickered on *Grasshopper.* Plowman answered with his dimmed signal lamp. It flickered again, and stopped. "*Grasshopper* turning to starboard, sir."

"Very good."

Grasshopper turned 180 degrees to starboard and headed back towards the entrance. E 11 went on alone.

"We'll dive in about an hour," Nasmith said. "Perhaps sooner if we're spotted."

D'Oyly nodded, went to the conning tower hatch and climbed

down through the circle of light. Of course their diesel engines would be heard on shore, but they were measuring out their lives by the endurance of the batteries and he dared not use them to run the almost silent electric motors until it was necessary to dive. He felt that every time the searchlight swept over them they would be picked up, that it would steady on them and the guns would open fire, but it never wavered nor stopped its regular movement. Probably the greatest danger was from the dark European shore where watchers by the batteries might see the conning tower silhouetted against the light.

The night was very clear: the black outline of the hills, which Nasmith had memorised from the drawings in the Admiralty Sailing Directions, was visible against the starlit sky. He was coming up to a slight depression in the hills which he identified as being opposite the mouth of the Suandere River where Boyle had been fired at. Although every mile gained on the surface would lessen the strain on the batteries, it was important also not to be seen at this early stage if it could be avoided: Nasmith decided to dive a little sooner than Boyle. The very powerful searchlight at Kephez, five miles higher up, was touching them also, and it seemed impossible that they could avoid detection any longer. As they drew abreast of Achi Baba at 3.50 a.m., and the approach of dawn was lightening the sky, he sent the helmsman to the steering position in the control room, and stopped the engines.

"Diving stations!" he ordered, not sounding the klaxons as it was important to avoid making a noise.

Down below, the coxswain and second coxswain ran to the hydroplane wheels. Supervised by D'Oyly, the men closed the ventilators, checked the hatches, switched on the air circulating fans and stood by the valves and manifolds, and Jupp struggled with the clutches disconnecting the diesels.

On the bridge, Nasmith took a final bearing and looked at his watch. When the report came from D'Oyly, "Both engine clutches out! Shut off for diving!" he nodded to Brown to go below. Then he sat for a moment on the hatch coaming with his feet on the upper rungs of the steel ladder, looking at the searchlights and visualising the course that he must now follow blind, then he went down also, shutting the lid after him. As he came down blinking into the glittering interior, and Wheeler reached up and closed the lower hatch of the conning tower shaft, he said to Brown, "We're about a mile off the European shore, Achi Baba abeam."

49

D'Oyly reported, "We're shut off for diving. All ready, sir." Brown read the log and noted the position on the chart.

"Start the motors," Nasmith ordered, for the coxswains at the hydroplane wheels could control her only when she had way on, then, "Flood main ballast."

He stood listening to the clang of metal on metal and the detailed routine orders echoing back and forth, "Open 1 and 2 Kingstons and 1 and 2 main vents!" "Number one full! Number two full!" "Flood three." Water roared into the tanks. "Open number 3 Kingston and number 3 main vent!" The bows dipped, and E 11 settled deeper in the water. When the gauge read 15 feet he adjusted the trim and ordered, "Take her down to 30 feet." They were now invisible from the shore and hidden from the eyes of the searchlights. Everything depended on his navigation.

When she was steady at 30 feet, he ordered, "Up periscope," and took a careful look all round. He could see nothing but the sweep and flash of searchlights and their reflection in the water. "Down periscope!" On Wheeler pressing a switch it slid back again with a swish and a creaking of wires. Nasmith turned to the coxswains, "Take her down to 80 feet," and he began flooding the forward auxiliary to help her down. He was roughly in the position where B 6 had been unable to go below 40 feet, but E 11 went down without any trouble. The position of the minefield ahead of them, and the depth at which the mines had been laid, was known only approximately. They nosed their way forward blindly at less than three knots to conserve the batteries and to avoid jarring the mine moorings more than was necessary. The hands, except for the four "diving hands" who were always at their posts while the boat was under way submerged, were allowed to fall out. They were served with steaming mugs of cocoa and some of them settled down to sleep, others to play cards or read – it was important that they should move as little as possible, for a man moving, particularly if he is doing energetic work, uses up oxgen at a far quicker rate than a man at rest. Nasmith remained watching the helmsman, Greene, to make sure he was always on the correct course, and the depth-gauge and hydroplane indicators to make sure that the correct depth and trim were being maintained. The log registered their speed through the water, but he had no means of estimating the speed and direction of the current.

Suddenly there was a metallic clang forward. They listened in dead silence as a mooring wire scraped along the outside of the hull. "Stop port," Nasmith snapped. The telegraph rang and the port propeller stopped. The helmsman turned his wheel to prevent her head from swinging off to port. D'Oyly put his empty cocoa cup down on the wardroom table, very gently, as if the slightest additional vibration might explode a mine. The wire seemed to be caught up for an instant on one of the propeller guards and then was thrown clear. "Ahead port. Plot the position," Nasmith said. The propeller revolved again and Brown read the log, looked at the time, and marked the estimated position of the first evidence that they were in the minefield.

More wires rasped along the hull, the sound greatly magnified by the water — it was like being inside a drum, for a submarine is itself a hydrophone, a receiver that vibrates to sound waves. Every time, Nasmith stopped the port or the starboard propeller to prevent it fouling the wire and perhaps dragging the mine down on to them. Then there was silence, except for the click and hum of the slow-running electric motors, the buzz of the small motors moving the hydroplanes and the occasional rattle of the steering gear. When they had heard no ominous scrapings on the hull for ten minutes, Nasmith decided to risk going up to periscope depth to find out where they were. The risk of striking a mine had to be accepted to avoid the greater risk of running aground. With barely an hour of darkness left, he didn't want to find himself high and dry on a sandbank like E 15. At 4.50 a.m. he ordered diving stations, to rise from eighty to thirty feet.

The depth-gauge showed seventy, sixty-five, sixty-four, sixty-three feet and then went back to seventy feet. "She's heavy, sir!" sang out the coxswain at the hydroplane wheels.

"How's the bubble?"

"She's horizontal, sir."

"Start the pump on the auxiliary, and send for Mr. D'Oyly-Hughes."

"Ay, ay, sir." The bubble in the spirit level trembled and moved slightly as D'Oyly came from forward to the control room: the boat was as delicately balanced fore and aft as a pair of scales. The pump started noisily.

"What's the trouble, D'Oyly?"

"Can't find a thing wrong, sir. Nothing to account for negative buoyancy, unless we've sprung a leak."

"I'm not going to blow main ballast till I have to, for she might surface — and that's what we mustn't do here. Put the hydroplanes hard a-rise, and we'll go full ahead for a few minutes."

"Both hard a-rise, sir." D'Oyly went forward again and Nasmith ordered full speed ahead on both motors. At great expense of battery power, E 11 drove forward and slowly began to rise. "Sixty feet, sir! Fifty . . . forty . . ."

"Full fields!" Nasmith slowed the motors down. "Hold her at thirty feet. Don't let her surface!"

"Ay, ay, sir. Thirty-four . . . thirty-one . . . twenty-eight . . . twenty-six . . . twenty-five . . ." It seemed she was going to surface after all.

"Hold her at thirty feet!"

"Ay, ay, sir." The coxswain and second coxswain sweated at the wheels of the hydroplanes, and at last she levelled off at thirty feet.

"Up periscope, slowly."

Wheeler carefully worked the switch controlling the periscope. Nasmith grasped the training handles as it rose and bent down to the eye-piece, leaning backwards in an effort to keep it low and prevent more than a few inches of it from protruding above the surface. He was almost blinded by the blaze of a searchlight. He shuffled round training the hooded lens in a complete circle, then ordered, "Down periscope," and to the coxswains, "Take her down. Seventy feet. Flood the auxiliary. Stand by the blows." To get her down quickly he flooded the forward trimming tank but began blowing again as he was going down and caught the trim at seventy feet. He went to the chart table, "We're here," he said, making a mark with a pencil. "Kephez is right abeam."

"But we can't be!" Brown said in astonishment. "Not for another hour. We've only made four knots through the water, and according to the chart there's been a two to four knot current against us."

"Yes, on the surface, but evidently there isn't any current at seventy feet."

Brown was still doubtful. "Could it be another searchlight?" he asked.

"What other one? We only know of three on the Asiatic side. Kum Kale we passed at the entrance, Erenkoy – and we can't be right in there, and Kephez, so it must be Kephez – but we're much too close to it."

"While we were trying to rise to periscope depth, we perhaps were being swept in towards it, as Brodie was." Brown was busy with parallel rulers and pencil. "If we're half a mile off the

52

searchlight now, course forty-eight degrees should clear Kilid Bahr."

Nasmith checked it carefully, for the Straits turn almost at right angles to port at Kilid Bahr, "Key of the Sea," which is on the European side, and at the same time they narrow to three quarters of a mile. D'Oyly came from forward with a worried expression. "I can't understand why she was heavy," he began, but Nasmith interrupted him cheerfully, "We're going to make it, D'Oyly! If we keep this up we won't have to surface in the Straits to recharge. We're off Kephez already!" He didn't want just then to discuss E 11's peculiar behaviour. He had been relieved of his greatest fear – that they wouldn't be able to get through against the current.

To avoid the dangerous set towards Kephez, he steered for the point of Kilid Bahr, on the other side, and bumped it at fifty feet – there was no danger of being stranded as he had plenty of water above him. He turned to port, slithered round the point and into the reach immediately below Nagara Point. She was soon in deep water again, and at 5.30 he rose to thirty feet – this time she came up quite easily – and had another look to make sure of his new course. The morning was getting lighter, and his periscope was immediately spotted and fired at: there was a loud report and the clang against the pressure hull of a shell bursting in the water. "That's all right," said Nasmith. "Roger Keyes doesn't care about guns."

"He doesn't care about guns?" said Brown. "What about us? Crikey!"

Nasmith retracted the periscope, went on up the Straits for ten minutes and tried again. It was considerably lighter now, and he could see three destroyers ahead who were evidently looking for him. They opened fire at the periscope, but, as they did so, he had a clear view up the reach beyond them of two battleships manœuvring in the direction of Nagara Point. "Down periscope. Man the bow tubes. Keep her at thirty feet." D'Oyly and the torpedo men hurried forward. It would have been difficult to find a trickier place than these narrow waters with swift surface current and unknown eddies, to carry out an attack. It was a pity that they had been spotted by the escorting destroyers, but there was not a breath of wind, and they could hardly have missed the white plume of spray thrown up by the periscope in the glassy sea. He had to guess what the battleships would do, assuming that they must have been warned by the destroyers that they were in danger.

"Two enemy battleships, must be *Turgut Reiss* and *Heirred-din Barbarossa,* bearing twenty degrees, distant two miles. They were steering 230 degrees. Time 2.30 p.m." Brown noted down all this information, and transferred it to his chart, to plot as far as possible the movements of the vessels.

Nasmith ordered the torpedoes in the bow tubes to be set to run deep so that they would do the maximum amount of damage to a battleship, and the torpedoes in the beam tubes to be set to run shallow in case one of the shallow draft destroyers had to be dealt with. One after another the torpedoes were swung back, the settings were adjusted, they were swung forward again into the firing position and the inner doors of the tubes closed.

"Flood the tubes!" Brown repeated the order through the voice-pipe to D'Oyly who echoed and implemented it, "Open the drains and vents! Air on the fore trim line!" There was a sharp hissing sound of air into the fore trimming tank forcing water into the tubes as E.RA. Brooker worked the spindles of the air manifold in the control room, followed by a cry of, "Tubes full, sir!" A rush of air amidships showed that the beam tubes were flooding. D'Oyly turned the wheel that released the bow caps at the outward end of the torpedo tubes, and threw them open by pressing on a lever. "Charge firing tanks!" he shouted, and a few moments later reported, "Both bow tubes ready, sir."

Nasmith increased speed – it would exhaust the batteries more quickly, but he had to try to get into position to attack. They could hear the thud-thud-thud of the destroyers' propellers approaching, roaring overhead, receding and approaching again. They were evidently working slowly upstream, estimating correctly what the submarine would do. There was no way to shake them off. Nagara Point lay ahead and a sharp right angle turn to starboard, requiring careful navigation: Nagara Point itself had to be given a wide berth, for it ends in a treacherous shoal with a swift current sweeping across it, and there might be under water obstructions in its vicinity also.

The next look through the periscope showed that the battleships were farther away, in full retreat up the Straits. They were making smoke, and they were right in the line of the sun which had now risen and was shining very bright and low with dazzling effect. With eyes streaming he ordered, "Down periscope," and carefully cleaning the lens with the chamois leather pad, he dictated to Brown, "Two battleships bearing ten degrees, distant three miles. They were steering about thirty degrees, evidently to round Nagara Point." It was disappointing that they had increased the distance between them, but he made light of it, "Well – they're going the same way as ourselves, so we'll follow them."

The destroyers were standing off Nagara Point, hoping, no doubt, that the submarine, following the battleships, would be caught in the swirl of the current there and get into trouble, but Nasmith, still looking upon the navigation as the greatest hazard, went right over to the European side of the channel, almost into Khelia Bay, before turning to eastward, and when he raised his periscope again he had rounded the bend and was well above Nagara Point. His periscope, as soon as it appeared, was greeted with such a furious cannonade that he could see nothing but spouts of water thrown up by the shells. He retracted it, and went on upstream, hoping that he was still following the battleships, but when he took another look, he saw that they had doubled back and were disappearing round Nagara Point at high speed on their way down the Straits. To follow them would mean abandoning his attempt to get through to the Marmara, which was clearly his first duty, so he had to admit defeat.

It was now 6.40 a.m. He reduced speed again and took E 11 down to seventy feet. He let the men fall out and relax, except for the diving hands, after closing the bow caps and draining the tubes. He sensed a feeling of let-down among his crew, which was only natural, but he couldn't help connecting it in his own mind with the last time he had had an enemy battleship in the sights of his periscope – he had got among the German High Seas Fleet, the dream of every submarine commander, on one of its raids into the North Sea. He had fired at a battleship at very close range, but as the torpedo left the tube, E 11 rolled heavily – it was a foul day – and he missed under. Before he could fire again, the battleship, travelling fast, was out of range. He had bitterly reproached himself, but on this occasion he had no need to: the Turks had handled their ships well, and had never given him a chance to get within striking distance. He told the men cheerfully that they would have another go at them on the way home.

At least they were through the Narrows, so the most difficult part of the Straits had been successfully negotiated – they were about in the position from which Stoker had sent his signal announcing his success. The final stretch of twenty miles should be easy going after what they had been through, for it was straight and never less than two miles across – so long as the batteries held out. The increase in speed to get round Nagara Point and stalk the battleships had exhausted them alarmingly. At frequent intervals D'Oyly tested the density of the electrolyte in the pilot cells and reported the results.

As the speed and direction of the current were still uncertain factors, Nasmith came to thirty feet every few miles to make sure he was on his course. The first time he raised the periscope, the current ripped against it, showering spray into the air and causing a foaming wake which streamed off at an angle from the wake of the hull of the submarine. He wondered what on earth they had picked up; perhaps they were towing a piece of wreckage that would give away their position, or even a mine mooring. He raised the periscope higher and got the bearing of a lighthouse on the European shore – a white iron framework on a hill – and of a solid stone lighthouse on the Asiatic shore which seemed to stand in the water. It was done in a few seconds. He recognised them at once as he had already seen them from the air. "Karakova Burnu forty-three degrees: Kudjuk Burnu ninety-six degrees," he called out to Brown who noted the bearings and transferred them to the chart. "Down periscope." It moved down quite freely: nothing had fouled the periscope anyway. Again they were farther up than they expected, a little to the European side. There was no possibility of a mistake: in those few seconds he had seen that the Straits were narrowing again, and he had picked up and identified the village of Bergaz with its mosque and three minarets. The hills on both sides were a delicate green with outcrops of purple limestone but there were more trees, and more cultivation, on the Asiatic side.

At 9.30 a.m. he raised the periscope again, and again there was the same effect of the wake of the periscope streaming off at an angle from the course of the submarine. He came to the conclusion that it was entirely due to the surface current taking a different course to the current round the hull which was thirty feet deeper in the water. He could see now, on the European side, the town of Gallipoli, which gives its name to the whole peninsula. It looked like a pile of white bricks on a green hillside. Farther up, a number of trawlers were patrolling in pairs, as if they were dragging wires along the bottom. He quickly took final bearings, retracted the periscope, and dived to ninety feet to pass below the Gallipoli minefield.

As the log clicked up mile after mile, the air became extremely foul. The men off duty slept or sat quietly reading. Those on duty moved as little as possible, partly because of the heat and

56

oppressive atmosphere, and partly because every additional effort caused them to breathe quickly and heavily. The air, which had not been renewed since they dived off Achi Baba nearly ten hours ago, was becoming exhausted of its oxygen and every man would have been sitting with a halo of poisoned air round his head if the circulating fans had not kept it constantly in motion. Their clothes were soaked with sweat. Moisture condensed and dribbled down the steel-plated sides of the hull, and even within the glass covers of the electric bulbs moisture collected and lay in heavy brown blobs that cast a shadow. Mingling with the all-pervading smell of oil, there was a sour smell from the batteries and from the unemptied sanitary buckets standing in rows behind the engines, for the heads could not be used when they were at a depth of more than thirty feet. Grey mist rose from the bilges, darkening the interior of the boat like a London fog.

At 1.30 p.m., according to their dead reckoning, they should have reached the end of the Straits where they open into the Sea of Marmara. Nasmith reduced speed to two knots, came up to fifty feet, called for silence and listened for the beat of propellers, knowing that every one would be an enemy. He heard none. He rose to twenty feet and pushed the periscope up into brilliant sunlight. There was no enemy in sight. They had gone well beyond the Straits into the Sea of Marmara which broadened out before him to a wide expanse to eastward. He turned the eye of his periscope towards the Asiatic shore, distant about five miles: pleasant wooded hills rose one above the other, higher and higher, towards range upon range of distant mountains. On the European shore, some three miles away, there was a barrier of steep barren hills with yellow cliffs sloping down to the sea. He didn't surface yet because he could have easily been sighted by coast watchers. He had strongly in mind the constant harrying of E 14 by enemy patrols while she was trying desperately to surface and recharge, and he thought it best not to draw attention to himself while his batteries were low. On the last of his electric power he went in slowly towards the European shore until the water became shallow enough for them to lie on the bottom. He took the boat down to fifty feet, then went dead slow on the motors and began flooding the tanks evenly and she gradually sank down, still with way on, and finally lay on the bottom with only a slight list to starboard in fourteen fathoms. He stopped the motors and took in another 200 gallons of water to weight her down and prevent her from drifting.

"Fall out diving stations!" For the first time since entering the Straits they could relax in comparative safety. The daily tot of rum was issued by the coxswain. The crew were warned to move as little as possible, so as to use the minimum amount of air. They lay down in a sort of stupor and slept by the light of a few dim yellow electric bulbs. D'Oyly and Jupp went slowly all through the boat, examining the hatches with an electric torch to make sure that all was secure and they had sustained no damage from grounding at Kilid Bahr, or from the shell bursts or the mooring wires in the minefields. Then Nasmith and the officers turned in also. Only a single watchman was left on duty to keep an eye on the depth-gauge and pressure-gauge, with orders to report immediately if there was the slightest movement.

FIVE

At 9 p.m., when Nasmith judged it would be dark enough to surface, he ordered diving stations. The air was thick so that a match wouldn't strike, and the interior was streaming with condensation. The men were wet through, grey-faced and breathing heavily, but the batteries had recovered sufficiently for him to go ahead slowly on the motors. Because he was afraid that any sudden effort might cause a heart injury, Nasmith gave instructions that his orders were to be carried out in slow motion. Blowing water from the tanks until they had positive buoyancy, they rose to thirty feet and Nasmith ordered, "Up periscope!" At first he could only see that it was bright moonlight, and then he could make out the line of the hills with vague shadows under them, but nothing moving, and no bow wave of a destroyer. He brought the boat up until only her conning tower was above water. Then he climbed up through the control room hatch and eased the conning tower hatch cover so that the air which had leaked into the interior from the compressed air system whistled out through the crack while the men all shouted to relieve the pressure on their ears. When Brown with his eye on the barometer called up to him that the interior and exterior pressures were equal, he threw open the hatch cover and clambered out on to the bridge with his night glasses. There was a dead calm. D'Oyly joined him. There was no sound except the barking of dogs coming distantly across the water. The signalman, Plow-

58

man, came up – he had the best eyes in the boat. None of them could see anything moving.

"We can charge now," Nasmith said. "Start with 500 in series. Be ready to break off. We may have to dive at any moment."

"Ay, ay, sir. We're all ready below."

D'Oyly disappeared again. They let the motors turn the diesel engines for a few moments without starting them: they sucked a stream of fresh air into the boat which cleared it immediately. The buckets were quickly emptied. The off-duty men turned in, and a look-out joined Nasmith on the bridge.

The port diesel started with a bang and a roar which sounded shattering in the still night. With tail clutch out so that the propeller wouldn't revolve with the shaft, it was geared to drive the port motor using it as a dynamo to charge the batteries. A few minutes later, as soon as they began to get a little power back into the batteries, they used the starboard motor to drive the boat slow ahead so that they would have control of her and be able to dive quickly if necessary.

Lohden, the W/T operator, came up to rig the wireless masts and aerial with Plowman. While waiting for darkness Nasmith had written out a signal, which Brown had coded, announcing their safe arrival in the Marmara. The range of their wireless set was only thirty miles, so the destroyer *Jed* had been stationed off Bulair in the Gulf of Xeros to keep listening watch so that they would only have to signal across the neck of the Gallipoli Peninsula to have their signals relayed to the flagship.

Meanwhile D'Oyly supervised the charge, keeping an eye on the ammeter as the revs increased. Almost immediately the klaxons sounded. "Diving stations! Break the charge! Close battery ventilators!" A destroyer was bearing down on them from the northward. As the sleeping men jumped up and ran to their diving stations, the engines stopped, and the look-out and Nasmith scrambled down into the control room.

D'Oyly reported, "We're shut off for diving, sir."

"Thirty feet!" Nasmith shouted to the coxswains, and then, "Flood one, two and three!" They still hadn't sufficient electric power to thrust the boat forward and downward in a crash dive. "Flood four! Flood the auxiliary!" They went down heavily and landed on the bottom again with a bump and a lurch. They shut the vents and stood listening to the roar of the approaching propellers. As sound travels through water at five times the velocity of sound through air, it was like a train rush-

59

ing across a viaduct. It passed and faded – they waited for it to return. They knew they were trapped if the destroyer circled in the vicinity to prevent them from surfacing and charging, but she held on her course, and the swish of propellers died away altogether. Either she hadn't sighted them or, not knowing that the submarine was practically unable to manœuvre under water, she was unwilling to risk being torpedoed in the clear moonlit night. Fifteen minutes later, E 11 surfaced again and continued charging.

At regular intervals D'Oyly tested the pilot cells, entering the readings of the density and temperature on the charging sheet and reporting them to Nasmith who remained on the bridge with the look-out. His spirits rose as the night wore on, and the moon swung low and dipped behind the hills. By midnight there was sufficient power in the batteries to increase their surface speed. They were still shut down for diving, with the helmsman steering from the control room. They carried so little buoyancy that the coxswains had to stay on the hydroplane wheels, keeping a little 'up-helm' on, to prevent the boat from diving accidentally.

At 0.30 a.m. the look-out gave a yell, pointed to a destroyer approaching from westward and dived for the hatch with Nasmith close behind him pausing only to sound the klaxons and bang the lid down after him and secure it. The charge was again broken and the diesel stopped. D'Oyly shouted to the coxswains, "Take her down!" as they had rehearsed so often. The coxswains turned the wheels, she dipped and was under in a few seconds. The gauge was at twenty feet as Nasmith landed in the control room. Again they listened to the rush of propellers above them – but this destroyer passed a short distance away, apparently without seeing them. When they surfaced ten minutes later, she was still vaguely in sight, disappearing to the eastward.

They made frequent attempts during the night to contact the destroyer *Jed* on the other side of the hills which lay before them. The range was short – not more than fifteen miles. Long blue sparks crackled off their aerial as their call sign went out again and again, but there was no reply. Nasmith was impatient as he wanted to relieve the anxiety of his friends and, in view of the uncertainties that lay ahead, he wanted to put it on record that at least they had succeeded in getting through to the Marmara. He told Lohden to make the signal without further delay, for he hoped that some other British ship would pick it up even if *Jed* didn't.

At 4 a.m., long before it was light enough for E 11 to be sighted from the shore, Nasmith broke off the charge, dived to periscope depth, and began to reconnoitre the western end of the Sea of Marmara. With fully charged batteries, E 11 was again an efficient fighting unit.

On the passage up through the Straits, only Nasmith had used the periscope. In the few fleeting glances which were all that he had been able to take, he had had to identify the leading marks and make his decisions without consulting his navigator, but now D'Oyly and Brown each took a periscope watch in turn, and Nasmith went to the wardroom. First he shaved – he was the only man on the boat to do so: it wasn't customary in The Trade to shave on patrol, and when chaffed about it he always said it was because he didn't like the prickly feeling of his muffler on his stubbly chin. He also changed into dry clothes: he hated wet clothes, and Petty Officer Greene, who looked after the officers, had improvised a drying cupboard for him, the source of heat being an electric light bulb in a tin.

Then, with a cup of coffee at his elbow, he pulled out the Admiralty chart of the Marmara and studied it thoughtfully. Now that the hazards of the passage up the Dardanelles had been overcome, he could devote all his attention to the real job that lay ahead – the cutting of the enemy's supply lines by sea to the Gallipoli Peninsula. He was well aware that the side which failed to supply its armies would inevitably lose, and that therefore the issue of the campaign might depend upon his own personal judgment and initiative, upon his making the right decisions and exploiting his favourable strategic position to the greatest advantage.

The Marmara is a very deep inland sea about 110 miles long and 46 broad, connected to the Black Sea by the narrow channel of the Bosphorus as it is connected to the Mediterranean by the channel of the Dardanelles. With these two channels it divides Europe from Asia. Its principal glory, the great city of Constantinople, or Stamboul, lies at its north-east corner where it is joined by the Bosphorus. It is almost entirely surrounded by mountainous country in which there are few roads and fewer railways, so that the most convenient method of transportation is by sea. The overland route available to the enemy from Constantinople, the principal source and centre of supplies, to their armies defending the Gallipoli Peninsula consisted of one railway on the northern side, going only part of the way, and one by a long detour on the southern side, also going only part of the

61

way, and two roads which in places were little better than mule tracks. Nearly all their supplies, therefore, were sent by sea, and it was to cut this supply line that E 11, E 14 and their less fortunate sisters, *Joule, Saphir,* E 15 and AE 2 had been sent on the hazardous journey up the Straits.

They found nothing at the entrance to the Dardanelles. As they turned and patrolled slowly eastward the sky grew lighter, and the calm water, at first a very dark blue, changed gradually to purple and then to a paler blue. At 5 a.m. they sighted Marmara Island and watched a dark orange-red sun rise directly behind its rocky peaks. Nasmith certainly expected to be hunted by numerous destroyers and gunboats as Boyle had been, but he saw none. He began a regular patrol between Marmara Island and the fine bluff headland of Kodja Burnu on the European shore, a distance of about twenty miles, because enemy supply ships would be almost bound to pass between these two points though there was a channel south of Marmara Island also, among the smaller islands of the same group. It was only three miles wide and was supposed to be used mostly by local sailing vessels. Hour after hour he patrolled between these two points, but sighted nothing – it was quite uncanny. He had imagined that the sea would be covered with ships hurrying to bring troops and supplies to the front line, and that they would be strongly escorted – to see none at all made him vaguely uneasy. Then, about noon, on approaching the European shore he saw a column of smoke on a headland, and then another a few miles farther on, and another, and he remembered Boyle saying that the enemy lit beacon fires by day and flares by night to warn all ships when a submarine broke into the Marmara. The coast looked as the south coast of England must have looked when the news was passed that the Spanish Armada had been sighted – he was reassured by this thought, and proud of his one-boat invasion, for it didn't matter that E 11 had found no targets for her torpedoes if her presence alone was interrupting and delaying the enemy's supplies. There was even a smoke signal on Marmara Island on a rugged precipitous slope near a marble quarry which gleamed white in the sunshine.

As it appeared that no ships were moving, Nasmith abandoned his patrol line and took E 11 along the coast to see if there were any in the anchorage off the important town of Rodosto, eight miles beyond Kodja Burnu. A light south-easterly breeze had sprung up, and the sea was rippling and sparkling in the sunshine, so they were able to approach at slow speed to within about a mile of the shore without much danger of their periscope being seen. The town looked very imposing: the sea front was a mile long, and houses and mosques of white Marmara stone spread far up the gentle slope of a hill among trees and gardens – but there was not a single ship in the anchorage. A long deserted iron pier jutted out into the bay, and even the fishing boats were all hauled up on to the beach. They moved in closer – looking through the high-power lens of the forward periscope was like looking through a pair of binoculars: they could see the traffic, and the people walking in the streets, and some girls on the sea front who seemed to be wearing white blouses and dark skirts. There was a dense crowd in front of a mosque near the shore. On a road leading out of the town a seemingly endless column of infantry tramped along with rifle and pack, with here and there an officer on horseback. They saw outriders clear the way for a train of artillery to pass them, with men lolling on the gun carriages, then a string of heavily-laden mules being hurried on in dust and confusion, then more infantry. Nasmith, D'Oyly and Brown all watched in turn. "Why haven't we got a gun? If only we had a gun!" they groaned to each other. It was tantalising to watch them pass and be powerless to do anything about it. The only consolation was that the troops had probably been disembarked because of the submarine scare and were faced with an exhausting march to reach Gallipoli.

Nasmith took E 11 out to sea and surfaced when they were twelve miles from the land. From this position they could survey a long stretch of the coast, but still there were no ships: nothing but a line of blue hills and a large flock of shearwaters lightly skimming the sparkling wavelets. They stopped the engines, disconnected the clutches and prepared to charge the batteries. When the charge was on, and look-outs posted, there was a welcome call of "Hands to bathe!" Three seamen, whose names were called out by the coxswain, threw off their clothes and plunged with enormous relief into the clear water. They were allowed to swim around for ten minutes, then they were recalled and the next three went in, and so on until everyone had had a turn.

Although the day had been entirely uneventful, and he hadn't exactly "run amuck in the Marmara," Nasmith was fairly satisfied. He thought patrols were few because every available ship had probably been sent out to hunt Stoker and Boyle, and now they were in port resting the crews, refuelling and repairing engine defects. He was glad of the respite, for his men had needed a quiet day after the strenuous passage of the Straits, and they had also been under a certain nervous strain while at Imbros waiting to start. The bathe had refreshed them. Cheerful laughter sounded forward and the gramophone churning out "A Little Love, a Little Kiss" mingled with the clatter of crockery as the cook prepared supper. He was cooking the last of the fresh meat and vegetables they had brought with them. The mess tables, slung above their heads, were unclipped and set up in the alleyway.

In the wardroom the conversation naturally returned to the possibility of interrupting the troop movements along the coast road. Nasmith agreed that the next time they came up they must have a gun, and promised that the first thing he would do when they got back to base would be to go alongside the first battle-wagon they sighted and persuade the captain to part with a four-inch, or at least a six-pounder. Then they could not only annoy the troops on shore but have a smack at some of the patrol craft and smaller vessels that were not worth a torpedo. "Of course," he said, "with a single small gun we couldn't do much against a column of troops. They would merely scatter, take cover and call up some artillery – whereupon we would have to dive and come up again somewhere else, loose off a few more rounds and dive again. We wouldn't be able to achieve much, but the nuisance value would be considerable."

"One really ought to go ashore," said D'Oyly, "and blow something up – a viaduct or an ammunition dump, or something like that."

"No, no!" Nasmith rejoined hastily, "I couldn't spare any men for adventures of that sort."

"But you could spare me."

"You least of all."

And there the matter rested, but Nasmith saw that his second-in-command had got hold of an idea, and that he would hear more about it.

At 3 a.m. on the following morning, when the charge was completed, E 11 dived and patrolled to the north-east. Sighting nothing, she surfaced again at 6 a.m. for hands to bathe, and to clean the boat. The weather was clear, and there was again a flat calm, but a bright luminous streak topped with grey cloud above the mountains to the east seemed to indicate a change. At 7 a.m. she dived and continued her patrol. A light breeze sprang up from the north-east accompanied by a slight haze which by ten o'clock had cut down visibility to about two miles and made observation by the periscope difficult. At eleven-thirty Brown, who was on watch, reported a vessel under sail. Nasmith had a look at her through the periscope and decided to investigate. He surfaced and studied his quarry through his binoculars with growing admiration. She was a two-masted sailing vessel with high bows and a broad beam that gave her at once attractive lines and good carrying capacity. She was large enough to be carrying military stores, heading for Gallipoli deeply laden and with all sail set to take advantage of the light north-easterly wind. She was built of wood and rigged like a ketch, but with an additional lateen sail reaching up like the wing of a swallow abaft the foresail. He increased speed to head her off, and shouted through the megaphone for her to heave to.

Seeing no way of escape, the Turkish captain lowered his sails with a run. Nasmith laid E 11 alongside and D'Oyly with an armed party jumped aboard of her. "No shoot good English!" the frightened captain shouted. There was a deck cargo of small logs of wood: D'Oyly indicated that he wanted some of them moved so that he could reach the hatch covers and inspect the hold. The mate and a boy ran to do his bidding – they were the entire crew – while the captain remained aft, guarded by Wheeler. "Don't shoot!" he said again, more hopefully this time, reassured by Wheeler's broad friendly grin. In spite of his scruffy beard and trailing moustache he was quite a handsome man with a very light, almost orange-coloured complexion, dark eyes and aquiline nose. He wore a fez, an old jacket and baggy trousers. The fez, a stiff round one, seemed to be a sign of his authority, for the mate had a soft shapeless one, a waistcoat over a striped shirt and the same kind of baggy trousers. The boy, who was about sixteen, also wore a soft fez, and a shirt and trousers that once had been white. The captain pulled out a packet of cigarettes and Wheeler, in the interests of good fellowship, accepted one but put it in his pocket as it was against orders to smoke while on duty and, as he said afterwards, he thought it might be drugged anyway.

Meanwhile E 11 was standing off. Nasmith studied the weather and didn't like the look of it, for the mist was closing in on them and making conditions as unfavourable as they could possibly be. The great advantage that a submarine has of remaining unseen and sighting an enemy at a distance is lost in poor visibility, and she herself is in constant danger of an enemy coming upon her unawares. A ship that would be an easy prey in clear weather becomes a deadly menace when her bows suddenly loom out of the mist. With this uncomfortable thought in mind, Nasmith waited for the boarding party to complete the search. If he submerged he would be able to see very little through his periscope, for it was a low-lying mist that seemed to cling to the surface of the water. He was considering the advisability of abandoning his patrol and diving to a safe depth when the idea occurred to him that he could use the sailing vessel as a stalking horse. He waited till D'Oyly hailed him and reported that no contraband had been found, and then he went alongside the sailing vessel again, made fast fore and aft with headline, stern-line and springs, and trimmed well down so that only the conning tower was above the surface. He sent a man up the vessel's mast, from the head of which there was a clearer view, to keep a look-out for enemy ships. "Hoist the sails!" he shouted through the megaphone. The order was implemented by a certain amount of pantomime from D'Oyly, and the Turks hoisted the sails with alacrity. "Coxswain to the ship's wheel!" was the next order, and then, "Hard a starboard, Coxswain!" E 11 went slow ahead, Dowell put the helm over, and the two ships swung round until they were heading due east and the submarine was completely screened from the shore by the sailing vessel. In this guise, changing the masthead look-outs every two hours, they sailed together eastward. The captain, having recommended everything to the guidance of Allah, seemed perfectly contented to be sailing away from his destination.

As they moved along slowly within the magic circle of their area of visibility which varied from a hundred yards to half a mile at sea level but allowed veiled sunlight to reach them from a luminous sky, Nasmith came aboard the sailing vessel and carried out a thorough survey with D'Oyly. They noted the soundness and thickness of her timbers, the capacity of her hold, which contained only logs of wood, how much fresh water she was carrying, and what provisions. They discussed what size of explosive charge would be required to sink such a vessel, and exactly where it should be placed. D'Oyly discovered four nice looking chickens which he confiscated, offering the captain a shilling for them which he politely refused. The chickens were sent aboard E 11.

During the afternoon the mist grew lighter, and they were able to study the coastline from the masthead through their binoculars. The Turks, having re-stowed the displaced logs, sat peacefully smoking. D'Oyly collected an odd assortment of empty paint drums, lengths of rope, spars and pieces of timber, and sent them aboard E 11. Again he offered the captain the shilling, and again it was refused. The crew were allowed, while off watch, to potter about the sailing vessel, exchange cigarettes with the Turks and carry on long conversations with them, of which neither side understood more than a word or two. At five-thirty the look-out reported that the white cliff of Deirmen Burnu was abeam. Brown went aloft to confirm their position. They were only half a mile off, and he could see an armed coast watcher standing on the cliff, looking out to sea, little knowing that the navigator of a submarine was looking back at him from the masthead of the sailing vessel. He may have thought it peculiar, however, that the sailing vessel was sailing directly into the wind. The two vessels now altered course, and headed out to sea.

At 6 p.m. Dowell came and reported that the Turks were making a signal fire to give away their position. Nasmith went aft and found that they had lit a smoking brazier on the poop and were preparing to grill some little bits of meat on a skewer. The smoke streamed upwards and could, no doubt, be seen from the shore, but he thought that no coast watcher would think there was anything unusual about it, and let them go on with their cooking. At 8 p.m. the fog lifted altogether. Nasmith cast off from the sailing vessel, signing to the captain that he was free to continue his voyage, which he did with many expressions of gratitude while the crew of E 11 sat down to a supper of roast chicken. During the whole day they had seen no other vessels except two distant trawlers and a gunboat.

Lohden, with Plowman the signalman to help him, had spent the day overhauling his wireless set. He had found nothing wrong with it, so Nasmith again headed west to get within range of *Jed*. The failure to make W/T contact was a constant source of annoyance as he knew that Roger Keyes, Brodie and his other friends must by now be seriously concerned for their safety. He had to restrain himself from blaming his W/T operator as the fault might well lie with *Jed*. The worst of it was that he couldn't repair a wireless transmitter himself. He prided himself that he knew as much about the engines, torpedoes, electrical installations and every piece of equipment on board as any of his crew, and could do any job in the boat in an emergency, and it was galling to find this serious omission in his qualifications. He felt that he had failed in his duty because, according to his code, he had to think of every possible emergency in advance. It was usual for a submarine commander to resent having to carry wireless, perhaps because, by tying him to the base, it restricted his freedom. Without it he would have an absolutely independent command: he resented the space it took up, and he resented having to carry another hand who was not required to work the boat. But Nasmith had always been interested in technical advances and, though conscious of the disadvantages, he would have preferred an efficient wireless. Particularly in the Marmara it was essential to be able to let the Admiral know what was happening, and in exchange he expected to get reports of the movements of enemy shipping. No doubt Lohden was a decent and conscientious fellow, but he wasn't a trained submariner: he belonged to a different organisation and had different loyalties. Next patrol he might be in a destroyer or a battlewagon, or at a shore station. He hadn't acquired the submariner's deftness and economy of movement, and his mess mates sensed that he was different. He seemed to them to swagger when he walked, like a cowboy wearing a ten gallon hat and a sixshooter. This impression, Nasmith very well knew was quite unfair. He mustn't allow himself to be prejudiced – the man had enough rudery to put up with from the rest of the crew – but the fact remained that he could permit nobody in E 11, even Lohden, to make a mistake.

During the night, at 3 a.m. on the 22nd May, they got within range of *Jed* again, being put down only once by an enemy destroyer on the way. They rigged the wireless mast, and for the next three hours tried to make contact – in vain.

SIX

At Mudros and Imbros, Nasmith had not said anything about his great ambition to be the first to enter Constantinople except to question Boyle on the subject, and he had been relieved to find that E 14 had not forestalled him. No doubt, as Boyle said and as Intelligence reported, it was well protected by mines, but as the port was in use and ships were constantly going in and out, there must be a way through them. There were reports also of mines in the approaches which could be fired electrically from the shore, and also of Brennan, or circling torpedoes which were believed to form part of the defences. There were batteries at Leander Point and at Seraglio Point on the opposite side commanding the entrance, and on the hills surrounding the harbour.

His first step must be to reconnoitre the approaches to be quite sure of what he was doing. He wanted to observe the exact route taken by the Turkish ships entering, which he must follow also to avoid the mines, and he wanted to gain more experience of the underwater currents which presumably would be particularly difficult to deal with in Constantinople Harbour into which the swift flowing Bosphorus pours vast quantities of water from the Black Sea, fed by the great rivers Volga and Danube and by the melting snows of the Caucasus.

After their second abortive attempt to contact the destroyer *Jed*, Nasmith again turned east. His intention this time was to continue his patrol right up to Constantinople. D'Oyly and Brown took watch and watch. They raised the periscope every ten minutes and scanned the horizon, but sighted nothing. The continued lack of targets when the ship's company were keyed up for action and excitement was most trying – but the Turkish ships would have to start moving again soon or leave their armies without supplies. At 4 p.m. they surfaced and had to crash dive immediately as they were attacked by a destroyer. When the coast was clear they came up again and continued eastward on the surface, charging as they went.

At 3 a.m. on Sunday the 23rd of May, Oxia Island loomed out of the darkness, a towering mass of rock 300 feet high. Here they altered course to northward and headed for Constantinople. As it grew light they saw the great city rising in the form of an amphitheatre from a grove of cypresses in the centre, with ancient walls along the water's edge and innumerable domes and minarets gleaming in the morning sun. A sailing ship passed ahead of them. They stopped her and were about to board when the look-out reported a steamer approaching from the westward. They dived immediately and tried to head her off, but she had sighted them. She ran for the shelter of the harbour and reached it before E 11 could attack. She was very large, with three masts, one funnel and clipper bow, probably an empty transport returning from Gallipoli. Carefully plotting her course for future reference, they returned to the sailing vessel which had got under way again. While D'Oyly and the boarding party were examining her for contraband, the look-out sighted a torpedo gunboat off the entrance to the harbour. "Bearing sixty-three degrees, sir," Brown said from the gyro repeater.

Nasmith closed the sailing vessel and called to D'Oyly to come back on board. With his two seamen he jumped on to E 11's bows as they touched the side of the vessel, and Nasmith signed

69

to the captain to carry on. As soon as they were clear, he sounded "Action stations."

Heading away from their target in case the sailing vessel should divine their intentions and contrive to give the alarm, he dived to thirty feet, then turned and headed for the gunboat. "Steer sixty-three degrees," he told the helmsman, and increased speed. He didn't intend this one to escape.

Every man stood at his post, tense with excitement. "Flood the bow tubes!" There was a hiss of compressed air forcing water out of the fore trimming tank — they had to be flooded from water already in the boat or the trim would be upset.

"Charge firing tanks." ... the details of the routine and trim he left to D'Oyly and his excellently trained crew and concentrated on the attack. For a minute or two there was intense activity all along the shining interior, and then D'Oyly's voice rang out. "Bow tubes ready, sir!"

He slowed down, and cautiously raised the periscope. The gunboat had dropped her anchor and showed no signs of activity. "Bring her up to twenty feet," he told the coxswain, "Steady now, she mustn't break surface." Nearer and nearer they crept. Eight hundred yards ... Seven hundred yards ... A slight adjustment to the course, then "Steady!" His sight, a thin vertical line across the lens was dead on the bridge. There was no deflection to allow as she wasn't moving. He couldn't miss if the torpedo ran true with its short range — high speed setting. "Stand by the starboard bow tube ... Fire!" There was a clatter and a thud as the torpedo left the tube, followed by a violent hissing sound of rushing water. The boat lurched, the coxswains spun their large wheels to keep the bow from rising before the tube refilled. The seconds ticked by, and then there was a dull BOOM! and a spontaneous shout from the men "Got her! Good old Nazims!" "Thirty seconds, sir," said Brown.

Nasmith took no notice, either of Brown or of the men. He remained standing with his eyes to the periscope, watching the effect of his first hit on an enemy warship. He saw the torpedo strike the gunboat amidships, and water and debris shoot up into the air, as she listed heavily to starboard. He smiled as he noticed a seaman run along the sloping deck of the doomed vessel to a gun and train it in his direction — what could he do now? The ship was obviously sinking! He saw the flash of the gun and heard a metallic clang against the hull of the submarine as the shell burst somewhere beyond her in the water. The seaman prepared to fire again ... suddenly there was a crash and the lens

70

went black before Nasmith's eyes as seawater rushed into the periscope – the Turk had hit it with his second, and last, shot. Only the lower lens, specially strengthened for just such an emergency, was preventing the water from flooding into the submarine.

"Down periscope!" he shouted. Nothing happened.

"Periscope's jammed, sir," came Wheeler's astonished voice.

"Take her down to thirty feet!" This would bring whatever remained of the periscope out of sight below the surface without, he hoped, putting too great a strain on the lower lens. "Hard astarboard. Half speed ahead!" He wanted to open the range, but as there was no more firing, he raised the second periscope, and saw the gunboat sink by the bows five minutes after she was hit.

Feeling rather like an assassin unexpectedly wounded by his victim, Nasmith abandoned the reconnaisance of Constantinople and headed out to sea, expecting destroyers to come out after him like angry wasps. When he had put a safe distance between himself and retribution, he brought E 11 to the surface to inspect the damage: he found that a six-pounder shell had passed clean through the upper tube of the forward periscope and practically severed it. As the wind was freshening from the north-east, he took shelter in the lee of the island of Kalolimno off the Gulf of Mudania on the southern side of the Marmara. It is a small island, long and narrow, so if the wind changed while they were busy with repairs, they would only have to shift to the other side. It seemed a pleasant enough place with hills rising to a conical peak and several villages and isolated monasteries – according to the Sailing Directions it was inhabited entirely by Greeks – the rough, broken land carefully terraced and cultivated, and it had only one tiny harbour – not large enough to conceal a hostile gunboat or destroyer. After circling round it and finding no other vessels in sight except a few fishing boats with light brown sails, E 11 anchored in ten fathoms with good holding ground about two miles off the western shore. This is one of the few places in the Marmara where it is not too deep for a submarine to lie on the bottom if necessary.

The immediate task now was to unscrew the top section of the damaged periscope – about four feet six inches long – where it protruded from the deck, and plug the hole securely. E.R.A. Brooker, one of the strongest men on board, undertook this task with Wheeler to assist him. The rest of the hands attended to minor repairs and adjustments, charged the batteries and cleaned

71

the boat. Brown tested the Sperry gyroscopic compass and wrote up the log while D'Oyly and the torpedomen reloaded the starboard tube.

The screw inside the periscope tube was very long, and the thread very fine, thirteen to one, packed with white lead. At first it seemed that it would be impossible to move it as they couldn't grip the tube firmly enough with any of the tools available. Among D'Oyly's treasures taken from the sailing vessel were an old oar and a length of grass rope. He cut off the blade of the oar, and with the loom and the grass rope he improvised a windlass which gave a very good purchase. While Brooker tried to turn the periscope with this improvised windlass, Wheeler played the flame of a blow lamp on to the lower part opposite the screw. They sweated, heaved and cursed in turn, but still it would not move. Then Nasmith told them to light a fire round it, which they did, feeding the fire with oily waste and the wood of the packing cases in which their tinned food was stored. At last, when they had been struggling for more than two hours, the white lead melted and Brooker succeeded in wrenching off the broken end of the periscope. They hammered a wooden plug into the hole with a heavy copper hammer until it was level with the top of the periscope standard, covered it with layers of canvas smeared with rubber solution and left it to dry. The broken top of the periscope was lowered through the conning tower hatch and stowed in the wardroom.

Having inspected the boat from stem to stern – the usual Sunday routine – and found everything in order, Nasmith called the hands to prayers and read the service. He could feel an excitement, a buoyancy, among them that naturally he shared, but at the same time he considered the damage to the periscope a great deal more serious for them than the loss of the gunboat for the enemy, for it might lead to the loss of E 11 and every soul in her. However, the men didn't see it in that light. For them, the important thing was that they had sunk an enemy warship at last. It was as if a jinx had been removed, a run of ill luck broken. It was a feeling that had its origin in the patrols they had made together in the North Sea in which success had always eluded them. As he passed among them before dinner, they looked at him with broad grins, he didn't exactly know why.

Apparently D'Oyly and Brown shared the feelings of the crew. When he drew aside the green curtains and entered the wardroom, he saw an array of beer bottles and an open box of cigars on the table. Then he remembered his vow, made months before, that he would neither smoke nor drink until he had sunk an enemy warship. D'Oyly and Brown jumped up, poured out three brimming glasses, and a cheer was heard from the mess decks.

Nasmith stepped out into the corridor again, glass in hand, and said "Thank you. I've got a wonderful crew!" and he drank to them.

Dinner was put on the tables, and they set to with a will. It consisted of hard tack hash, which was bully beef cooked with crumbled ship's biscuits. Jupp in the P.O.'s mess could be heard telling for the umpteenth time, the story of their most fateful North Sea Patrol. They all knew it as well as he did, but it was appropriate to the occasion so they listened ... "When the Huns had bombarded Scarborough," he said, "there was nothing to stop them from getting home again – the Fleet being in Scapa – except our submarines on patrol. In E 11 we found ourselves right in the path of their returning squadrons. Nasmith got into position to attack a battle cruiser, but as he was about to fire, she altered course towards us. Still he fired – it was the only chance now, but the boat got caught in a nasty swell and rolled to starboard. So we missed under. 'Bad luck, sir,' I said. We never got another chance. He looks at me, and he says, 'It's just as well I missed. She was too close. We would have both gone up together. But I'll tell you this, Jupp, I won't smoke or drink till I've sunk an enemy warship.' And no more he has."

There was silence for a minute, then Dowell spoke, "You heard what he said just now? I've got a wonderful crew? You don't know the rest of that story. Only him and me knows."

"What do you mean?" said Brooker. "What story?"

"Listen, and I'll tell you. It was at Stokes Bay, way back before the war. He was in command of D 4 at the time. Well, there was to be an exercise – we was to fire a practice torpedo at a destroyer, and I don't rightly know for why, but Old Nazims misses by a mile, and him with the best periscope eye in The Trade. It's well-known he has."

"And what happened?" Brooker asked.

"What d'you mean, what happened? Why, nothing happened. That night he says to me, 'Dowell,' he said, 'I've got a wonderful crew, but you've got a rotten skipper.' "

"But just now he didn't say, 'You've got a rotten skipper.' "

Dowell looked at him pityingly. "Explaining to some people," he said with a disdainful sniff, "is like sewing canvas with a bloody marline-spike," and he turned back to his dinner.

The rest of the Sunday was devoted to Swedish Drill and bathing. So that they could get in again quickly, the fore hatch was left open, but not the strongback supporting it made of girders continuing the curve of the hull, for the crew could pass between them, and it was difficult to close quickly. Nasmith acted as Swedish Drill Instructor, standing on the conning tower with the seamen lined up on the superstructure in front of him and the stokers behind. Then they were free to lark around in the water, playing their favourite game of diving from the conning tower on one side, swimming under the submarine and coming up on the other side. D'Oyly and a couple of seamen constructed a raft of the old timbers and paint drums he had collected from the sailing vessel. As soon as it was finished, one of them climbed on to it and immediately it capsized amid great laughter, but D'Oyly explained that it was not meant to carry a man. The idea was to swim and push it in front of you. Its cargo, besides some clothes, was to be a charge of guncotton and a firing pistol which could thus be conveyed ashore at dead of night without them getting wet, to blow up the Berlin to Baghdad Railway.

Their sport was interrupted by a call from the look-out, "Ship approaching Green Two O, sir!"

Nasmith was out of the water in a moment, shouting, "Everybody out! Stand by the weight! Break the charge! Diving stations!"

As the men scrambled aboard, the klaxons sounding, tumbled down the fore hatch and conning tower hatch and ran to the diving stations, most of them naked, Brown and Nasmith examined the approaching vessel through binoculars.

"Dive on the weight, sir?"

"No. Heave it in."

"Tail clutches in. Shut off for diving." D'Oyly reported from below.

"Fore hatch secured?"

"Ay, ay sir."

"Heave in the weight!" Brown shouted, and with a rasping sound the thirty fathom long wire began to wind round the small capstan – it was a small mushroom-like anchor that could be lowered from within the submarine even while submerged.

"She's only a small ship – not worth a torpedo," Nasmith decided, "and she's not going to pass very close, I doubt if we could catch her. We'll dive till she's gone by, as she won't have seen us yet. Tell the men to get some clothes on and return at once to their diving stations."

74

"Ay, ay, sir." Brown passed on the order, then pointed to D'Oyly's raft, "What about that thing, sir?"

"We can pick it up later. Stand by to dive. Flood one. Stand by two and three. Slow ahead both." They climbed down the hatch. E 11 sank lower in the water and then disappeared. The raft floated idly away. When they surfaced an hour later, the steamer had passed out of sight, and the raft was nowhere to be seen. It was a mystery what had happened to it. D'Oyly looked disgustedly at some fishing boats making for the shore, "Fishermen are all alike," he said. "They've got no respect for other people's property."

Nasmith now headed for the signalling billet at the western end of the Marmara. It had become even more urgent to get in touch with *Jed,* for they were badly handicapped by the loss of the periscope, and he wanted to make a signal asking for a new top to be flown out to him by one of Commander Samson's "hydro-aeroplanes" which were based at Tenedos. He knew that it couldn't be brought by submarine, at least for some weeks, as the only survivor of the flotilla – Boyle's E 14 – had gone to Malta for a refit.

The wind had fallen, and it was a beautiful starlit night. Nasmith took the first watch, from 8 p.m. till midnight. With batteries fully charged, they were running on the surface using the electric motors, with lower deck control – they were trimmed deep, the helmsman steering from the control room as though the boat were submerged. The coxswain was at the hydroplane wheel in case she should take a slant forward and go under, and in a few seconds he could take her down to invisible depths if necessary. It was a state of readiness that appealed to Nasmith. The events of the day, so satisfactory, as it appeared, to everyone else on board, were causing him grave anxiety. Naturally the crew were elated at having sunk a gunboat whose business it was to sink them, but the problem of attacking during the rest of the patrol with only one periscope, and of getting them all safely home again, was his alone. He sighed, and wished he could smoke another of the cigars which D'Oyly and Brown had so thoughtfully, and so optimistically, provided, but it was too late to smoke now – the glowing end would be visible for several miles and might betray them. That was the penalty for having meals at the traditional hours – he could never smoke after supper. No one had thought of blaming him for the loss of the periscope. Even to D'Oyly and Brown it had seemed an accident that could not have been avoided; but he had yielded to the temptation of

75

watching the death throes of his first kill when it would have been better to retract the periscope and dive deeper immediately after firing. These few seconds of idle curiosity had cost him his periscope and with it, perhaps, the success of his mission and the lives of his crew who were so ready to cheer him. As a result, their survival depended now upon a single fragile eye of glass. He had overheard Jupp's story, and it brought back vividly the emotions of that memorable day with the excitement – and the disappointment – that he would never forget. It had started one evening in December with the beam of a searchlight in the sky, signalling in plain language, "Eighth Flotilla close," when E 11 was returning from a patrol. He closed the searchlight, with due caution, and found Commodore Keyes in the destroyer *Lurcher* who sent pencilled orders across to him in a dinghy – the German Fleet was at sea! He was to intercept it at the mouth of the Weser. The next morning a heavy swell had come up, making depth keeping difficult, but at 7.20 a.m. he sighted many destroyers on a broad front approaching from the northward. He went deeper and let them pass overhead, and then three large columns of smoke appeared which slowly developed into three enemy battleships. More and more ships appeared, eleven battleships and battle cruisers, zig-zagging and in no apparent formation, but all bearing down towards the Weser entrance. With both bow tubes at the ready, he went in to attack a battleship – but just as the sights were coming on, she altered course towards him. He made an alteration of eight points to prevent her from getting any closer, brought the starboard beam tube to bear, and fired at approximately 250 yards. The torpedo could not have missed for deflection at that range, but there was no explosion. It must have run deep and passed beneath her. He turned to attack the next battleship, which was very near, but she too altered course, this time straight towards him. To avoid being rammed he dived to 70 feet, flooding his internal tanks to increase the speed of his descent. As he hit the bottom, she thundered over him – the terrific WOOMF! WOOMF! WOOMF! of her huge propellers made E 11 tremble. He could still hear it. Immediately she had passed, he blew ballast – he was exactly one minute on the bottom – and tried to come to periscope depth in her wake to attack the next one, but E 11 came whirling to the surface and lay in full view of the enemy ships. As if by pre-arranged signal, they all turned their sterns towards him – it was hopeless to attack again. He had lost his chance. He followed them up the Weser Channel and ran aground ... but all that was past. He was in the Marmara now, at the gates of Constantinople. If he had not accomplished much in the first four days of the patrol it was because he had wanted to reconnoitre, to get the measure of his enemies. Well, he had the measure of them now!

The Turks were very wide awake, skilful in manœuvre and damnably good shots. He would have to get up very early in the morning to get to windward of them . . . and then the curious idea came to him that he would literally get up earlier than the Turks: he had only to put the clocks on an hour, perhaps more – and he smiled to himself, for it occurred to him that with supper an hour and a half earlier he could enjoy an after supper cigar on the bridge while it was still daylight.

These lonely vigils were a necessity to him as a relief from the petty vexations, the responsibilities from which he was never free, and particularly from the knowledge that thirty men were constantly watching him and judging from his behaviour, his attitudes, his every expression, whether things were going well or ill; and as long as he appeared cheerful and confident, they would be also. Alone on the bridge he could relax and allow all his worries, so resolutely dispelled during the day, to flood back into his consciousness and sort themselves out. He soon began to feel at peace. The bridge was a tiny moving island on the boundless sea under the all-embracing sky where the stars had their destinies just as he had. Only here could he escape from the glittering steel cylinder in which he had condemned himself to live, and be part of the night.

At 2 a.m. on Monday the 24th of May, E 11 got within W/T range of *Jed* once more. She crept in towards the north shore of the Marmara until she could establish her position by a fix on the dark outline of the mountain peak of Elia Tepe and on Mal Tepe farther west. Engines were stopped, and the wireless masts rigged. Nasmith handed over to Brown, telling him to send word at once if the operator was able to make contact, and went below. He hadn't been ten minutes in the wardroom when Lohden knocked and entered:

"I've made contact with *Jed*, sir."

"Are you sure? Reception clear?"

"Yessir."

"What's been the matter all this time?"

"We found a defect, sir, in the aerial."

"In OUR aerial?"

"Yessir. Where it comes through the deck, an oil cup should have been filled, and – wasn't. I'm sorry, sir."

Nasmith was silent, pale with anger, but when he spoke at last, all he said was, "It's lucky for you we're both equally to blame. I should have known how to put it right." He picked up a sheaf of signals which Brown had coded in readiness, and selected one. "Get this off first," he said, "it's about the new periscope; and then this one – the report of our activities. Then accept anything they want to make to us. After that, we'll pass the remainder if there's time. Off you go now – full speed! We must be out of here before daylight – that gives you less than three hours."

"Ay, ay, sir." And the very relieved W/T operator hurried off with the signals. He had expected at least to be shot at dawn.

Nasmith felt it as a personal disgrace that a defect anywhere in E 11 had gone undetected for four days, but he was thankful that the annoyance of returning again and again to the signalling billet, and failing to make contact, was over. A number of signals came through during the night but, when Brown had decoded them, they amounted to very little. The most serious was a report that B 11 patrolling off Smyrna had sighted a U Boat. This was the first appearance of a U Boat in the Mediterranean. When the more urgent signals had been exchanged, they asked *Jed* for news of land operations, but all they got back was, "Heavy fighting continues."

At 5 a.m. they dismantled the wireless mast and got under way. The clocks had been put on during the night so that the whole ship's routine was forward one and a half hours. It was a glorious day, the sky clear blue with a few fleecy clouds, the sea calm. The hills rising abruptly from the coastal plain receded gradually in a wide sweep to the north. Nasmith had decided on a more aggressive policy: he patrolled on the surface now, and he was determined to let no ships get past him to Gallipoli; and if he should find no ships at sea he meant to seek them in every harbour along the coast and finally in Constantinople. With a sudden rush a school of porpoises broke surface half a mile ahead, flinging themselves high into the air, catching the sun for an instant on their gleaming sides, cascading down into the sea again. As suddenly, they vanished. Then their long torpedo-shaped bodies, clearly visible in the limpid water, shot under the bows of the submarine and broke surface again half a mile astern.

At 6 a.m. they sighted smoke on the horizon and increased speed to investigate: but it drew away from them, and disappeared. At least it was evidence that ships were moving. Then, at ten o'clock, they sighted a small steamer approaching from the east and heading directly for them. They dived, and Nasmith studied her carefully through the periscope: she was deep in the water, evidently with a heavy cargo, and she didn't appear to be armed. He brought E 11 to the surface on her port quarter, climbed out of the conning tower hatch with a megaphone, and shouted to her to stop. The captain took no notice, except to alter course away from the submarine. Nasmith called for a rifle, and fired several rounds at her bridge. She slowed down, and E 11 began to overhaul her.

"Abandon ship!" he shouted through the megaphone, "Abandon ship!" and his voice rang across the intervening space. They must have understood him and expected a torpedo to follow, for there was sudden pandemonium. The captain left the bridge – the ship was still going ahead with engines at half speed – and some of the crew ran to the lifeboats. They lowered one, but it immediately capsized, as the ship still had way on, and the occupants were thrown into the sea. Then a surprising number of men appeared on deck. Some threw themselves overboard, others rushed for the two remaining lifeboats with the result that a second one went down unevenly and capsized also – the wake of the steamer was bobbing with heads and waving arms. Nasmith took E 11 up to the first capsized lifeboat, and stopped while D'Oyly and the seamen righted it and pulled some of the Turks out of the water to man it – fortunately they were wearing cork lifebelts. Then he went ahead to overtake the steamer. As he came alongside her, a solitary figure stepped out on to the deck from one of the cabins, leaned over the rail and shouted in broad American, "Good morning, Captain. I'm pleased to meet you!"

"Go and stop the engines!" Nasmith shouted back.

The American went below. In a few minutes the engines stopped, and he appeared on deck again. He was wearing a checked knickerbocker suit with a white waistcoat and bright yellow boots. He waved his hand cheerfully, "How d'ye do, folks? Glad to meet you all!"

"What ship is that?" D'Oyly asked from the bows of the submarine.

"*Nagara*, out of Constantinople, for Chanak with Turkish marines."

"Any war contraband aboard?"

The American paused and lit a cigar. "Well," he drawled, "I'm not sure. I haven't really examined the cargo. Excuse me a minute." He walked to the third lifeboat and managed to restore order sufficiently for it to be swung out and lowered without mishap while D'Oyly and three armed seamen leapt aboard the steamer to examine the cargo. The first thing they found was a six-inch gun barrel lashed diagonally across the foredeck under a big tarpaulin. The fore hold contained a six-inch gun mounting and several twelve-pounder pedestals. The after hold was full of six-inch shells and, on top of them, fifty large size white metal cartridge cases, charges for the big fifteen-inch guns. They were all marked "Krupps" with the trademark of three interlocking circles.

D'Oyly came back and reported to Nasmith who said, "Right. We'll blow her up. Set the charge low down against the ship's side in the after hold – but first get the captain's charts and papers."

Shouting to the leading torpedoman to prepare the charge, D'Olyly took more men aboard the steamer. They whipped through the captain's cabin, the stores, the living accommodation, and came back not only with the ship's papers, but with an extraordinary collection of loot – eggs, chickens, potatoes, barricoes of fresh water, butter, clothes, boots, a medicine chest, a typewriter, (these last items evidently from the American's cabin), a varied assortment of souvenirs including a board with the ship's name on it in Turkish, and boxes of cigarettes.

Meanwhile the American who had been helping to right the second capsized lifeboat, left the Turks baling it out with their fezes, and came back on board still smoking his cigar. He approached D'Oyly. "I'm Raymond Gram Swing, of the *Chicago Herald,*" he said, with outstretched hand.

"What did he say?" Nasmith asked.

"He's a Mr. Swing," D'Oyly repeated. "Newspaper man."

"I want your story, Captain," Mr. Swing went on. "The whole of America will want to hear about this."

"There will be plenty of stories to come," D'Oyly said. "We're sinking all Turkish vessels, except hospital ships."

"How many submarines have you got in the Marmara?"

"Eleven!" said D'Oyly laughing – it was the first number that came into his mind. "Didn't you really notice any war contraband in this ship?"

"The United States is strictly neutral," he said with a twinkle.

"Tell him to get to hell out of it! Tell him the ship's going to blow up!" Nasmith shouted, exasperated at the delay, for the look-out had reported a second ship approaching from the east.

"O.K., Captain – we'll meet some other time, shall we? It'll be a pleasure. Good day to you, gentlemen!" and with another friendly wave of his hand, he returned to the Turks in the lifeboats, and they set off on their long row to the shore which was about three miles distant.

Nasmith studied the second ship through his binoculars: she was a steamer similar in size and type to the one they were dealing with, and she also was deeply laden. He waited impatiently till the Turks in the lifeboats were well clear, then he turned to the coxswain, "Are all the men back on board?"

"Yes, sir. All present and correct, sir."

Nasmith nodded to D'Oyly who went back on to the steamer with the leading torpedoman carrying a demolition charge. They placed it in the after hold as Nasmith had directed – 16½ lb. of guncotton, well tamped with six-inch shells and fifteen-inch cartridge cases. The leading torpedoman came back to E 11 first, and they all waited in silence. Then D'Oyly appeared, running like a hare, and jumped on to the bows of the submarine. They went full astern on the motors, and backed away from the doomed ship. The fuse was set to fire in four minutes, and they were hardly out of danger when the charge detonated with a loud report, a column of smoke and flame shot up, the decks lifted bodily and shells and cartridges were hurled in all directions. The ship heeled over, cocked her bows into the air and, in a few seconds, disappeared. "That," Brown commented, "in the words of the prophet, was certainly some sink!"

Two live ducks surfaced among the debris and solemnly swam away in the direction of the shore, following the lifeboats. D'Oyly watched them sadly. "How did I miss the ducks?" he asked. "Where the hell were they?"

SEVEN

Before the smoke had cleared over *Nagara*'s grave, E 11 had dived and was stalking her next quarry. The approaching steamer held on her course for a few minutes as though nothing had happened, but she was evidently uneasy, for instead of heading directly for the scene of the explosion she altered course a few degrees so as to pass to southward of it. Then, as if suddenly aware of her danger, she altered course again, this time to northward, increased speed and headed for Rodosto.

Nasmith, abandoning all further attempt at concealment, surfaced and headed after her at full speed, gradually decreasing the distance between them. Smoke rolled and billowed from the steamer's single tall funnel as the stokers tried to force another half knot out of her, and she kept up a succession of violent blasts on her siren. After a while it became apparent that she was going to reach Rodosto first, but as Nasmith had reconnoitred the place only three days before, he was sure that she couldn't escape him – and if the crew managed to get ashore before he torpedoed her, so much the better: it was the ship and her cargo that he was after, not the men.

As pursuer and pursued drew near to the shore there was considerable activity in the town. People could be seen hurrying away from the sea front, and others hurrying down to it. An officer was leading a column of troops on to the long iron pier that jutted out into the bay. As on the previous occasion, there were troops on the road leading out of the town: some halted and turned back, others pressed on. Nasmith, as he approached, scanned the confusion to see if any guns were being placed in position to fire at him, but saw none.

The steamer lurched alongside the end of the pier. She was evidently carrying munitions also, for the crew, hurriedly securing her, abandoned ship and ran away from her along the pier, meeting the troops coming out to defend her, and stopping their advance. She was deeply laden, and her decks were piled high with packing cases.

"What water is there?" Nasmith asked.

"Barely six fathoms, sir."

"That will do." He sounded the klaxons for diving stations and slowed down to two knots. "Flood the bow tubes and charge firing tanks."

There was a crackle of rifle fire from the pier as E 11 slid under the surface. A few minutes later she touched the bottom. He took her in slowly, bumping along the sand: he meant to get close enough to make certain of a hit, but the water became so shallow that a considerable portion of the periscope had to be exposed. At 1,000 yards from the target he ordered, "Stand by bow tubes ..." and a minute or so later, "Fire!" They waited in suspense, and then the ship blew up with a terrific report in smoke and flames. He could watch with a good conscience this time, as he couldn't retract the periscope any farther. She seemed to disintegrate, and the end of the pier was shattered with her.

After a minute of complete silence, rifle fire broke out again from farther along the pier and from along the sea front. Nasmith ordered, "Slow astern both!" and E 11 scraped out along the bottom, gradually finding deeper water, but not before a rifle bullet had clanged against the exposed tube of the periscope.

As soon as they were out of range, they surfaced and anxiously inspected it. There was a dent in the lower section of the periscope tube where a bullet had lodged in the brass – fortunately it was not in the thinner upper tube where it probably would have penetrated. They extracted the bullet, and the periscope could still move freely up and down. They submerged and continued the patrol.

"Two torpedoes gone, and three ships sunk!" said D'Oyly, hugely delighted. "Fine work, Skipper!"

"Lay off a course, Brown," said Nasmith dryly, "for Constantinople. We'd better get in there while we still have a periscope."

Diving out of the bay, they sighted smoke again, and a course was made towards it. It gradually resolved itself into a paddle steamer heading towards Rodosto.

"You'd better re-load the starboard torpedo tube," Nasmith told D'Oyly, "but this looks more like a job for a demolition charge. Shallow draft, no cargo-carrying capacity, probably a ferry boat. Can only have a deck cargo – or troops. You'll have to put the charge against the side of the ship in the engine-room."

While the leading torpedoman and stokers lifted another polished, shining torpedo from its rack, and lowered it into the starboard tube, E 11 slowly approached the unsuspecting paddle steamer which made a rapid, heavy thud – thud – thud, as her paddles churned the water and drove her forward. Nasmith surfaced, being careful to keep on her quarter, and hailed her through the megaphone to stop. She immediately did so. Her decks were heaped with coils of barbed wire, and there were also a few horses.

"Abandon ship!" he shouted through the megaphone, then "Stand by, boarding party. Warn Mr. D'Oyly-Hughes, and tell the L.T.O. to get a demolition charge ready."

"She's moving again, sir!" Brown shouted suddenly.

The steamer, going ahead on one paddle, and astern on the other, swung round until she was bows on to the submarine, then she came straight for her, her paddles madly thrashing the water.

Nasmith pushed the klaxon button and shouted, "Full ahead both! Lively now!" and E 11 drew ahead just in time to clear the vicious bows of the paddler.

83

Although she had failed to ram the submarine, she had gained some distance by this manœuvre. Before E 11 could turn to pursue her, she was half a mile ahead, racing for the shore, steering a sig-zag course and making all the smoke she could.

Nasmith called up both the seamen's and the stokers' firing parties. "Get that man at the wheel!" he shouted. They levelled their rifles, and opened a brisk fire on the steamer ahead. The helmsman left the wheel and made a dash for the shelter of the bridge. The steamer swung off her course and presented the whole length of her starboard side.

"Flood torpedo tubes! Charge firing tank! Swing bow caps!"

"Forward torpedo tubes ready!" D'Oyly reported, but before Nasmith could give the order to fire, the helmsman had rushed back to the wheel and got her on her course again, presenting only the narrow target of her swaying stern to the submarine.

"Where are all you Bisley marksmen? Seamen versus stokers!' The volleys crashed out again. Again the helmsman was driven from the wheel and the steamer swung broadside on, but he came back and saved her again. The shore was only five miles distant, a line of low sandy cliffs with grassland rising beyond them to the hills, and the helmsman never left his wheel for long enough to let the steamer present a fair mark for a torpedo. When E 11 closed on her again, she turned to ram and drove straight at her, forcing Nasmith to take rapid avoiding action. At last she reached the coastline, ran straight up on to the beach and stuck fast, her paddles still churning and forcing her bows deeper into the sand. Her crew leapt overboard into the surf and swam and scrambled ashore. Some tried desperately to scale the crumbling cliffs, while others raced away along the beach.

"What water in there?" Nasmith asked.

"Her stern must be in about eighteen to twenty feet, sir."

"What's the bottom?"

"Mud until close in, then sand and shell."

"We'll try to put you aboard, D'Oyly. Take the L.T.O. and three men, and work fast."

E 11 grounded long before she reached the steamer. They blew ballast tanks to lighten her, and crept in farther. At last they edged her bows up the steamer's stern, against the stream of water thrust back by the thrashing paddles.

D'Oyly and his men were about to jump aboard her with a demolition charge when two horsemen appeared riding furiously along the top of the cliff, followed by a troop of cavalry at full gallop, perhaps fifty strong.

"Drive those fellows off!" shouted Nasmith, and his seamen and stokers opened fire on the horsemen. Several fell, but the remainder threw themselves from their horses, unslung their rifles, spread out in open order, lay down, and fired volley after volley at the submarine.

"Firing parties stand fast! Everyone else below!" Nasmith ordered, as bullets rattled against the stanchions and conning tower. The seamen and stokers continued the action, taking such cover as was available, but their antagonists were now scarcely visible. When the conning tower hatch was clear, Nasmith said, "As I call your names, go below one at a time. Wheeler . . . Brassington . . . Baker . . . Mayne . ." They ran and tumbled down the hatch, happily without casualties. Then Nasmith followed them. As he turned and gave a last glance at the steamer which would now escape him, a bullet zipped through his uniform cap. He bobbed down and closed the lid. "Diving stations!" he called. The klaxons sounded. The clutches were thrust in, the vents closed. "Shut off for diving sir."

"Slow astern both," he ordered. " 'Midships." After hesitating for a few moments, E 11 tugged her bows out of the sand and slowly retreated, all praying that the periscope wouldn't get another hit. They had to bump for a half a mile over the shallows with bullets smacking against the conning tower before they could submerge. In order to waste no time in getting under, they reversed the controls and dived stern first.

"Well, there's no harm done," said Nasmith cheerily. He was mightily relieved to have got all his men down below without casualties. "He's got some guts, that Turkish skipper. He'll get his ship off to-night and deliver his barbed wire safely and he deserves to. But I never thought E 11 would be chased off by a troop of cavalry!" He looked long and thoughtfully through the periscope. "I can't let them get away with that. I think I'll take a smack at her . . ." It would be a long shot at a tiny mark, as only the stern and the paddle boxes on either side were visible – if he had gone to one side to open the target up he would have been too far away. Was it worth risking a torpedo? He was haunted by a vision of the Turkish front line with that deck cargo of barbed wire extended along it.

"Imagine their faces," said Brown, "if the ship blows up now before their eyes!"

"Flood the stern tube."

"Ay, ay sir. Stern tube ready, sir."

He took his time about the shot, and only when he was satis-

85

fied that the stern tube was absolutely dead on, he gave the order, "Fire!"

The track appeared to run straight for the steamer ... but it passed harmlessly along her port side and the torpedo exploded on the beach. Either his aim had not been true, or, at the last moment it had been deflected by the slipstream of the racing paddle wheels. "Probably frightened the horses," he said disgustedly. "Sole effect of a torpedo worth a thousand quid." Obviously being chased off by cavalry still rankled.

It was now 3.30 p.m. They steered south-east to draw away from the coast. Brown took over the periscope watch, but no more ships were sighted. At 5 p.m. they surfaced. A thorough inspection revealed no damage more serious than dents and scratches.

"Hands to bathe!" It had been a long and sweltering day, and this moment had been eagerly awaited. There was nothing in sight but the distant blue range of hills to the northward, so Nasmith let a whole watch go in at a time while he gave the other fifteen minutes of Swedish Drill.

After their swim they were all ready for their evening meal, most of them not even remembering that it was being served an hour and half earlier than usual. In addition to the usual fare there were eggs, butter, raisins and Turkish cigarettes from the ammunition ship they had blown up that morning.

Meanwhile the batteries were charging, and again Nasmith and D'Oyly visited every corner of the boat and heard the detailed report of every Petty Officer on the operations of the day.

"What was the name of that ship?" said Brown, stabbing away at Mr. Swing's typewriter on the wardroom table. "I want to put it in my report. It sounded like a cross between a cough and a sneeze."

"I thought you would want to know that," D'Oyly said laughing, "so I brought you her name plate," and he produced a board with some Turkish writing on it.

Brown looked at it casually. "Ah yes, *Nagara*. Very thoughtful of you. Thanks, old boy," and he stabbed again at the machine. Brown had picked up various scraps of miscellaneous information in his travels in the merchant service, including it appeared, some knowledge of the Turkish alphabet, or perhaps he had just remembered the name. "This typewriter ribbon is a bit worn," he went on. "You didn't think of looking to see if Mr. Swing had a spare?"

"Is that right – *Nagara*?" asked D'Oyly, rather crestfallen.

"Yes," said Nasmith, "that's what he told us. Same as Nagara in the Narrows where the battleships gave us the slip."

"Well, that's some consolation anyway." D'Oyly stowed the Turkish board beside the top of the broken periscope.

"Must hand it to the Yankee," Brown said. "He deserves full marks for his coolness. How's this?" He quoted from his half-written report. ". . . A gentleman appeared who said he was glad to know us all. He introduced himself as 'Swing' of the . . . what was it? *The New York Times*? That'll do anyway. . . .'"

"Sounds all wrong to me," D'Oyly interrupted. "You can't just say Swing. Americans always have a name, then an initial and then another name. What about Alfred E – no. Try Silas Q. Lots of Americans are Silas Q."

". . . who introduced himself as Sila Q. Swing. That's better. Sounds fine!"

"What did you make of the six-inch gun, D'Oyly?" Nasmith asked.

"Well, it was German. So was the ammunition."

"I wonder if it was one of the *Goeben's* guns? That might be important. It would show that the Turks were short of guns, and were pressing the Germans for them. But the Germans wouldn't give up any of the *Goeben's* guns without a struggle unless they didn't mean to bring her out again."

"Then you think we'll find her in Constantinople?"

"Not a hope. Latest reports say she was in the Black Sea. And even Turkish warships don't lie in the harbour at Constantinople. They take them through the Galata Bridge into the Golden Horn where we can't follow them – unless they've left the gate open, which isn't likely."

"Anyway," said Brown, "It's nice to feel we may have sunk one of the *Goeben's* guns, even if we can't sink the *Goeben*."

Nasmith took advantage of the extra one and a half hours of daylight to go up on to the bridge to smoke a cigar and review the events of the day undisturbed by the chatter in the ward-room. The air felt cool and fresh. The sun was already low, blazing across the sea and turning it to liquid gold. There was no wind, and the boat rolled easily in a gentle swell as she drifted aimlessly with the current. There was no other vessel in sight. As usual he dismissed the look-out so that he could be alone with his thoughts. He could hear the laughter of the men below, the tinny gramophone, the hum of a motor, voices raised in argument, the sudden clang of a hammer. He lit a cigar and inhaled the curly smoke with evident enjoyment, feeling that he had earned it, and yet, the more he thought about it, the less he was satisfied with that day's work. The men had behaved very well, as they would, naturally, but their marksmanship had not been good enough to prevent the paddle steamer from escaping, though they were expert at hitting tins and bottles bobbing up and down in the water. He would have to devise some other kind of target practice if he had to rely on rifles for stopping ships. Altogether, the first day of getting up earlier than the Turks had not been an unqualified success, because it seemed that some of the Turks had got up earlier than he had – the cavalry, and the captain of the paddle steamer. The biggest mistake of all had been the waste of a torpedo, and it was only now that he realised fully what a serious mistake it was. In North Sea patrols the average was about one hit for the expenditure of three torpedoes, but that was nothing to go by. The situation here was quite different. The effort to get them here had cost so many lives. Nearly thirty torpedoes had been lost in E 15, AE 2 and *Joule,* so the value of one that had been got through to the Marmara was infinitely greater than one at the base. He could not excuse himself for having expended on the difficult target presented by the stern of the paddle steamer, a torpedo capable of sinking the *Barbarossa.* The whole incident was untidy and unsatisfactory; he had felt it to be so at the time, and it was his attempt to tidy it up, to finish it off neatly and dramatically, that had made him risk that parting shot. He should have broken off the engagement and retired while the honours were even, but that is always a difficult thing to do, particularly for a man who has been trained never to accept defeat. It was a job for a gun really. If he had had even a six-pounder, the paddle steamer would never have got away. On the other hand, if the Turks had brought up a gun with their cavalry, E 11 would never have got away. Historically, it was almost a unique case of an engagement between a submarine and a troop of cavalry, and no doubt the sympathies of historians would be with the cavalry who had saved the steamer from inevitable destruction by preventing the demolition party from boarding her, and so were Nasmith's sympathies when he considered the affair as a detached observer. He also greatly admired the initiative and the skill and gallant bearing of the Turkish skipper. It was very curious, the difference in the nervousness of the crews of the vessels he had attacked, the behaviour of the first two making the determination of the third rather unexpected. The psychological effect of the sudden appearance of a submarine could evidently be very powerful, but not in all cases. The big test would be the sudden appearance of his submarine in the middle of Constantinople Harbour, if he could manage to get in. The moral effect and feeling of defence-lessness might be important factors in undermining the Turk's will to resist, it might cause difficulties for the Turkish Government, and it would certainly disorganise the transport of troops and supplies to the front. Its geographical position had kept the capital secure from attack for so many hundred years: the shock of the breaching of the defences might be considerable. The propaganda value, the prestige value for Britain, would be enormous. He could imagine Mr. Swing writing a stirring account of the incident "for the whole of America" – though he would have to borrow a typewriter. What an outcry there would be against the Government at home if a U Boat were to sail up the Thames and torpedo a ship in the Pool of London! It would be more prudent, of course, to carry out a routine patrol, it was all that was expected of him, submerging when an enemy destroyer appeared and attacking when an enemy battleship or supply ship appeared, but this could not satisfy him. He believed that the essence of successful naval warfare, and particularly of submarine warfare, was to do the unexpected, to seize the initiative, and the great prize lying before him was Constantinople.

He was still alone on the bridge when the sun set beneath a cloud and threw up a lurid glow like the distant flames of a burning city. He threw away the stump of his cigar, summoned the look-out, and went below.

He joined D'Oyly and Brown in the wardroom where the charts of Constantinople Harbour and approaches were spread out on the table. For the hundredth time they studied the leading marks and soundings, and tried to visualise the contours of the bottom and the probable force and direction of the currents, for that was the most serious problem. Again only surface currents were given, and they were sufficiently perplexing. The Admiralty Pilot said: "... where the main current from the Bosphorus and the counter-current meet they produce violent reactions which sheer vessels in all directions...." What went on below the surface at the depths at which they would have to operate, they could only guess.

At 10.30 p.m. they got under way, and proceeded towards Constantinople.

EIGHT

All through the night they headed eastward, and at 6.30 a.m., Nasmith time, on the following day, Tuesday the 25th of May, hands were called to prayers under the conning tower. It was then only five o'clock, but the daily routine started. When the sun rose above the mountains ahead of them, they were abreast of Oxia Island, around which in a blaze of light myriads of seabirds screamed. Beyond it lay more rocks and islands, rugged and bright red, partly shadowed with pine trees, and then range after range of the mountains of Asia, the most distant white with snow.

The two sides of the Marmara were closing in, almost to meet at Constantinople lying on the shores of the Bosphorus, but the hills on the European side were hidden in mist. E 11 dived to periscope depth, and headed north. A light breeze ruffled the surface, and sometimes green water momentarily blotted out Nasmith's view through the periscope. As she approached the European shore, the mist cleared. The city with its hundred glowing domes and ancient encircling walls with flanking towers, seemed to rise out of the sea. The walls, though partly in ruins, surrounded the oldest part of the city which lay on a promontory formed by the Sea of Marmara on one side and the long estuary, the famous Golden Horn, on the other. The white close-packed, red-roofed houses were dwarfed by the splendid mosques and palaces. On the converging Asiatic shore of the Marmara there were white villas, mosques and gardens with lilac-coloured trees and dark-green cypresses, and several piers for ferry steamers.

There were no ships entering or leaving the harbour, but there were many brown-sailed fishing boats and dhows, so Nasmith only raised the periscope every ten minutes for a quick look to establish his position. At noon, still undetected, he was one mile south of the large, square Marmara Tower at an angle of the walls where they come down the hillside and turn to run along the sea front. He followed them for three miles towards Seraglio Point. Innumerable small craft lay under the walls, gaily painted, with swaying masts and spars, and here and there a coloured sail. People were crowding along the road behind them with carts and pack donkeys – and there was a little closed cab like a box on wheels.

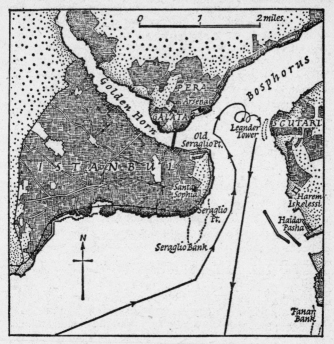

Constantinople harbour, showing the route of E 11

They were nearing the harbour entrance and, although no target was yet in sight, Nasmith ordered, "Flood the tubes!" and listened with grim anticipation as his order was repeated and amplified by D'Oyly forward. Soon the report came back, "Bow tubes ready, sir!" Everything must be ready in advance, for he meant to torpedo the first sizeable target he sighted, and make his way out again as quickly as possible. Keeping a mile offshore to skirt the Seraglio Bank, he altered course to port when the dome of St. Sophia was bearing due north, rounded Seraglio Point, marked by a prominent white lighthouse, and entered the Bosphorus: this was the track followed by the steamer they had observed entering on the day they sunk the gunboat, so he reckoned it would be clear of mines.

He was now passing between Europe and Asia, here only a mile apart. When he pushed the periscope up for a few seconds, he could see on his right, on the Asiatic shore, the big Haidar Pasha terminus and docks, and then the old town of Scutari with cranes and grain elevators, and the square Leander Tower standing on a rocky island. On the European side he was only a quarter of a mile from the city walls. He kept the boat at twenty feet, being anxious not to get into the uncharted deep currents – if she lost her trim and surfaced here, it would mean disaster. He cleared Old Seraglio Point, turned again to port and entered the main harbour of Constantinople. His first object was to see if the German battle cruiser *Goeben* and her attendant light cruiser *Breslau* were in the harbour, but this object he kept to himself. He felt that if any of the others knew that he hoped to find her, and she was not there, whatever else they might achieve would fall short of their expectations. Therefore he had always argued that *Goeben* couldn't possibly be there, that she was being used in the Black Sea against the Russians, or that she had been passed through the Galata Bridge to the naval harbour in the Golden Horn. The bridge consisted of masonry arches resting on iron pontoons: the centre sections were movable to allow warships to pass through.

Soon he was surrounded by harbour service craft, and he pushed up the periscope for the briefest possible glimpses as he threaded his way between them. There were ferry boats, tugs, launches, strings of barges. . . . Once he raised it close to a dhow and found himself looking into the face of the captain standing on the poop with arms folded. At the same instant the captain saw the periscope. His mouth opened in astonishment, and then he hurriedly looked away as if trying to imagine he hadn't seen it. If he had looked again, he would have seen only a swirl of water. The next time the periscope came up, it was a few feet from the stern of a Turkish Admiral's barge which had just passed overhead, and it quickly went down again to be pushed up stealthily a quarter of a mile farther on – and this time it wasn't retracted. Wheeler, beside him, saw the line of Nasmith's mouth harden, "Cruiser at anchor," he snapped out. "Bearing twenty-eight degrees. Distance five hundred yards. Charge firing tanks. Open bow caps! Port ten . . . steady!" The orders were repeated with a ring of excitement in the men's voices. Nasmith gazed intently through the eye-piece. "Full fields! watch the depth . . ."

The motors slowed down as the torpedomen working at the motor switchboards in the after compartment increased the fields to give the maximum resistance.

"All ready for'ard, sir!" D'Oyly shouted. Brown stretched out his hand to the firing levers . . .

Suddenly Nasmith straightened up. "Hold everything!" he shouted. "Down periscope. Starboard twenty. Take her down to thirty feet. Steady as she goes." Then he looked at Brown. "I nearly did it," he gasped, "and then I caught sight of her flag. She's American!"

"Thirty feet, sir," came from the coxswain. Nasmith blinked and wiped his eyes. "Up periscope, Wheeler, slowly." He put his eyes to the lens again, and altered course to port in order to give the cruiser a wide berth. He negotiated a line of mooring buoys, and then had a closer view of the Galata Bridge, the centre section closed. *Goeben* may have been lying in safety on the other side of it, but she was definitely not in the harbour. He selected as his target a large transport lying at the quay in front of Topkhana Arsenal – the main Turkish Army barracks and stores. There was a smaller vessel lying ahead of her, and he thought he might get them both with a left and right. There was little room to manœuvre, and the boat sheered off to starboard where the main current of the Bosphorus met a counter-current. He brought her up to twenty feet, steadied her, took aim at the larger of the two vessels and, making due allowance for the current, fired the port bow tube. The torpedo rushed off at a tangent, leapt into the air, flopped back into the sea and disappeared. ". . . capsized gyro," he muttered to himself, and immediately fired the starboard bow tube. He observed the track running straight for the large transport. He also observed the track of another torpedo heading straight for him.

"Full ahead both! Seventy-five feet!" he shouted. "Flood the auxiliary! Take her down! Quick!" They dived deeper just in time. The torpedo rushed overhead and circled towards the inner harbour where it found its mark and exploded somewhere in the direction of the Galata Bridge. An instant later there was another heavy BOOM! as his second torpedo struck the ship at the Arsenal Quay.

"Hard aport!" He longed to rise to periscope depth again, to observe the effect of his shot, but as the shore defences had evidently sighted him, and the reports that they had Brennan torpedoes – that could be guided by wires from the shore on to a target – were unpleasantly confirmed by the near miss, it would have been foolhardy to risk letting them sight him again and send another torpedo after him.

"Slow ahead," he said. "Stop the auxiliary pump. Hold her at seventy-five feet," and then to Brown, "Course for the entrance?"

"One hundred and thirty-five degrees for half a mile, then one hundred and eighty, sir. We're in twenty fathoms."

"Steer one hundred and thirty-five degrees," he said to the helmsman, and slowed down to two knots. He had achieved his object in torpedoing a ship in Constantinople Harbour, and now he must get his men safely out of it again. The enemy guns opened up, and the impact of shell bursts in the water hammered against the pressure hull. Some fragments, or perhaps a handful of shrapnel, rattled against it like dried peas.

"That was bloody close!" said Wheeler involuntarily, and then straightened up as he caught Nasmith's cold eye fixed upon him.

"Any more chaps like you, Wheeler, where you came from?"

"Yes, sir — I don't know, sir."

"Then get on with your job."

"Yes, sir," and he grabbed a stanchion as the boat rolled and swung to port, caught by a deep swirl of the current. The helmsman struggled to get her back on her course.

Suddenly the coxswain sang out, "She's rising, sir! Sixty-five feet — sixty feet — fifty-five — she's rising fast, sir!"

"Keep her down! Hydroplanes hard down! Full ahead both! Flood the auxiliary! Helm amidships."

"Hydroplanes hard a-down, sir. 'Midships, sir."

The pump started. The water hissed and rushed into the tank. "Gauge reading?"

"Fifty feet, sir." The rising movement had been checked.

"Course one hundred and thirty-five degrees. Stop auxiliary pump."

"She won't answer, sir. Swinging to starboard," the helmsman reported.

"Stop port! Hold her at fifty feet! Helm amidships."

"Going down, sir. She's heavy, sir — can't hold her!" shouted the coxswain, labouring at his wheel. "Sixty feet, sir. Swinging to port, sir," reported the helmsman.

"Stop starboard! Hydroplanes hard a-rise! Blow the auxiliary! Full ahead both."

"Course one hundred and eighty degrees now, sir," said Brown, looking up from his chart.

"Right. Steady on one hundred and eighty degrees. How's the bubble?"

"She's five degrees down by the head, sir. Gauge reading

seventy feet, sir. Still going down . . . Seventy-three . . . Seventy-five . . ."

The helmsman got her on to her new course, but couldn't hold her there. She seemed to be passing through an enormous seething cauldron. The orders followed each other in rapid succession – too quick for Brown, working at his chart and notebook, to record them all – one rapped out almost before the crew had had time to repeat back and carry out the one before, as Nasmith strove to regain control, and, above all, to prevent her coming to the surface. She rose, she went deep, she swung to one side and then to the other, lurching and rolling so that the men had to cling on to the wheels and manifolds to keep their feet. There was a sudden jolt and a loud scraping noise as the current drove her ashore. There was sixty feet on the gauge. Still the current drove her on, and she bumped up to fifty feet, then forty feet: in another moment her periscope and conning tower would be above the water.

"Full astern both! Flood main ballast. Flood 1, 2, 3 and 4." The auxiliary had just been blown at pressure and couldn't be used at short notice, but the forward movement was checked, and she settled firmly on to the bottom in forty feet. "Shut off the blow. Stop both."

"Six tons extra ballast, sir," D'Oyly reported. The men wiped their streaming faces. Brown went on working at his chart. There was silence except for the shell bursts in the water, some far away, some near: apparently the gunners were firing at random with no idea where the submarine had got to. Nasmith didn't know either. Presumably, as they had been making for the entrance, they must be on one side of it or the other, either on Old Seraglio Point or on Leander Point. There was a harbour defence battery on each of them, so he couldn't show his periscope to find out.

He blew the forward trim into the after trim and back again to see if she would tilt up and perhaps slide off into deep water. He tried again and again: it was useless. She was steady as a rock He must blow the extra ballast they had taken in. Then she would come off the bottom and, without rising more than a few feet, he must head for the open sea – but where was it? If he headed the wrong way, the boat would drive farther up the beach and lie under one of the batteries like a stranded whale. She would end as E 15 had ended at Kephez. He mustn't make a mistake – all their lives depended on it. He turned to Brown who was still bent over the chart table, "Do you know where we are?" he asked, but Brown shook his head. No effort of calculation could help them much after what they had been through, for they couldn't tell how far they had drifted, or in what direction.

Nasmith's mind was alert for any indication that would help him to decide. The men were all looking at him. He glanced at the compass – the ship's head was S.S.E. He ran up the steel ladder to the conning tower scuttles, opened one, and then the other, and peered out through the thick glass at the water outside: he thought it should be slightly lighter on the seaward side, but he could detect no difference. As he stood there for a moment, swallowing his disappointment, a little fish swam up and peered back at him through the glass. He closed the scuttles, went down again and looked at the chart, but he knew every inch of it already and it was useless unless he knew where he was. The guns, that had been tearing up the surface of the harbour for half an hour, were silent. It probably meant that the patrol boats were out searching methodically for them, with their long sweeps fitted with explosive charges dragging along the bottom.

He went and stood before the compass. He must decide now – but there was nothing upon which to base his decision. Feeling that with his own unaided strength he couldn't solve the problem, he closed his eyes for a moment, and felt a gentle movement as if a hand were rocking the boat. He opened them with renewed hope, and saw that the compass needle was stirring. He watched it, fascinated.

"She's swinging, sir!" said D'Oyly beside him. The current had caught her again, and was turning her on her own axis.

"South-east," the Helmsman chanted, then "East-south-east ... East ... East-north-east ... North-east ... Nor' nor' east ..." and then more quickly as the current came on the other bow, "North, Nor' nor' west, North-West...." Without speaking or moving, Nasmith watched the compass needle turn a complete circle as the boat swung round, and he knew they were delivered. By some extraordinary chance she had grounded precisely amidships and as the current gripped her again she was swinging anti-clockwise, and it must be strongest to the westward of him so he was not on Seraglio but on Leander Point, on the foul ground under the old Leander Tower.

"Diving stations!" he rapped out, recalling his crew to their duties, and every man laid his hand ready for the orders that would follow. He waited until she headed south-west again, then "Blow 1, 2, 3, 4, 5 and 6!" and as soon as the powerful pumps began to drive out the water from the tanks and she rose off the bottom, "Full ahead both! Hydroplanes hard down! Keep her on the bottom! Stop the blow!"

The depth-gauge needle went round to fifty feet, and then sixty, immediately confirming, to Nasmith's joy, that they were going in the right direction – away from the shore. They went on gently bumping down to eighty-five feet on the bottom. "Keep her at eighty-five feet," he ordered. "Half speed ahead. Course 190 degrees." She found her diving trim, and went on steadily and easily towards the centre of the channel. Without showing the top of the conning tower, without even raising the periscope, he steered her confidently out of the harbour.

Twenty minutes later he brought her up to thirty feet, "Up periscope!" They were well outside the entrance. "Dome of St. Sophia bearing 306 degrees. Chamlija Tepe sixty-nine," he announced.

Brown marked the position on the chart, "I can't tell you how relieved I am, sir!"

"Take over, Brown, will you? Steer south-west, and call me when we're out of sight of land. Take a look around every ten minutes – and you can fall out diving stations. Let me know if you sight anything larger than a fishing boat."

"Ay, ay, sir."

Nasmith went aft, chatting to the men on the way, to make sure they were all happy, then forward again to the wardroom where he sat down. D'Oyly joined him, and Greene brought cups of coffee. "Take one to Mr. Brown, will you?" "Ay, ay, sir."

They sipped their coffee for some minutes in silence, then: "There's one thing I don't understand," said D'Oyly, as if he understood everything else. "What the hell went wrong with our first torpedo?"

"Something wrong with the gyro. She never got on her course or found her level. Jumped right out of the water and rushed off, God knows where. In fact I'm wondering if the Turks really fired a Brennan torpedo, or was it our own that came back at us?"

"What? Our own torpedo that nearly did for us? How do you make that out?"

"Well, the time would have been about right – ours must still have been on the move; and then, if the Turks had really fired a Brennan at us, it would have been set to run deeper, to pass under their own ships and yet hit a submarine."

"Isn't that the bloody limit? The L.T.O. will have a fit. We've checked the gyros a dozen times. It must have been a defective one. And of course it won't be the Admiralty's fault. It never is. They'll blame us for it."

"It's the first time I've been glad of a miss!'"

"It's bad enough to waste a torpedo – but to torpedo ourselves. . . !'"

"If it frightened the Turks as much as it frightened me when I saw it coming for us," said Nasmith smiling at D'Oyly's indignation, "it can hardly be called a wasted torpedo. It circled twice round the harbour – must have scared the life out of all the other ships – as they had no idea where it was coming from – and it certainly hit something. There were definitely two explosions. I wonder what it was?"

"It must have been terrifying, with the guns firing and shells churning up the surface of the water all over the place. And then, to torpedo a ship alongside the main arsenal! I can't see any troopships or ammunition ships sailing from Constantinople for at least a week."

"Yes . . . There may be fewer targets for a while."

"Just as well." D'Oyly stretched out his long legs comfortably. "The men need a rest."

"The first thing," Nasmith said firmly, "is to reload the bow tubes – but we'll have to make some adjustments first and overhaul the gyros of the remaining torpedoes."

"To-day?"

"Of course. We don't want another one to go berserk."

D'Oyly looked at him thoughtfully, "And then, I suppose, we make for the signalling billet to get the signal off that will announce to the world that Constantinople is no longer impregnable and inviolate. What a great moment! It will justify everything you have done. I want you to know how happy I am for you."

"Thanks," he said. "I think it justifies all of us. You'll get your chance too one day, I'm sure. Naturally, as we've scored at least a prestige victory, it's important to let the Admiralty know about it as soon as possible."

There hadn't been the slightest trace of envy or reproach in D'Oyly's voice. It was as if he understood that Nasmith's highest ambition was not so much a desire for fame as a determination to live up to a stern conception of duty, to live up to a tradition. Neither was there anything in Nasmith's manner or appearance to arouse envy. He did not at all look like a man who had just succeeded in his greatest ambition, perhaps because he was not conceited enough to think that he should take all the credit himself for the success of their exploit, or for their deliverance. He had been at a loss to know what to do and that was a chastening thought for a man who had striven by his own efforts and efficiency to overcome an adverse fate.

"Are you feeling all right?" D'Oyly's voice interrupted his meditation.

"Oh yes. Fine. Perhaps I need a shave ..." He rubbed his chin, got up and looked at himself in the small mirror above the folding basin. At once he understood the reason for D'Oyly's question. His face looked immobile, like a mask, with exaggerated lines, and an unhealthy pallor showed beneath the suntan below his eyes and round his mouth.

"Would you do something for me?" D'Oyly went on. "Before deciding definitely to reload the tubes, to overhaul the gyros and to make at once for the signalling billet, would you take a walk with me through the boat?"

"Something wrong?"

"No, nothing wrong at all. The men have done a tremendous job, all of them, and they're feeling on top of the world. They know as well as we do that they've taken part in a unique operation, something they'll be able to boast of for the rest of their lives. I'm not questioning their willingness – they'll do anything you ask of them, you know that – I'm questioning their efficiency. They're over-tired, almost light-headed, some of them. Look at the strain they've been under – not only to-day – think of yesterday, it wasn't an easy day either. In fact they've had little chance to relax since we began the patrol more than a week ago. . . ."

"All right. Let's go." Nasmith cut him short.

They walked together along the corridor which was lined with the sprawling forms of exhausted men asleep. In the control room, Brown, with his eyes to the lens of the periscope, jumped when Nasmith addressed him, "Anything in sight?"

"No, sir. Only the range of hills to the north."

Nasmith took a look also, and passed on. The only other occupants of the control room were the helmsman, who stood stolid and immobile, never taking his eyes off the compass, and the second coxswain, Kirkcaldy, working the forward hydroplane wheel with an effort of concentration, though the boat was running easily in perfect trim.

Aft, in the engine-room, more off-duty men were lying asleep, covered with dirty oilskins to keep the drops of moisture off them. Two men over an unfinished game of cards were talking in low excited voices. On all of them he recognised the same masks, the same kind of set expressions on their faces he had seen on his own face in the mirror. After more than nine hours diving, the fog rising from the bilges gave the scene an unreal, even a nightmarish look, and over everything was the nauseating smell of oil and dirty sweat-soaked clothing. As he walked slowly round, talking to a man here and there, he realised what D'Oyly had been getting at. He hadn't meant that it was the men's efficiency that was impaired, but Nasmith's own. His intention, it was clear, had been to warn Nasmith that he was driving himself too hard – not only the men – and now that he realised the danger, he felt grateful to D'Oyly for pulling him up. He knew very well that a tired man under nervous strain is apt to be reckless, or else too slow in his reactions, when faced with sudden emergency and, much as he disliked the idea, he had to admit that his own judgment might be impaired after the prolonged strain to which he had subjected himself.

At 3.30 p.m. he surfaced and gave the order, "Hands to bathe."

As Nasmith thought it likely that the enemy, finding that he had escaped, would send destroyers to search for him, and possibly aeroplanes, he would let only three men bathe at a time. It seemed only natural that the Turks would react strongly, and make a great effort to find and destroy the submarine that had struck such a blow at the very heart of their empire, and he didn't intend to be caught napping. Dowell, who, except for Plowman, had the keenest eyes in the boat, and could be trusted not to let himself be distracted by the antics of the bathers, he posted as look-out.

As he stood, watch in hand, on the bridge, he was astonished to see Wheeler rise up in the water, shout for help and swim like a madman back to the boat, followed smartly by his two companions, David Greene and Bonner.

"What on earth's the matter?" he asked.

"Sharks, sir," said Wheeler panting.

"Nonsense. There aren't any sharks in the Marmara. You're dreaming!"

"No, sir. Some hard thing pushed against me, like a big log, it was, sir. I thought it was my mates having a lark – but I looked and saw they were nowhere near. So then I knew – a shark, sir!"

At that moment a large dolphin leapt out of the water in a

cascade of silver spray, plopped gracefully head first back again, and dived under the boat.

"There! It's only a dolphin. He wants to play with you, Wheeler."

They all laughed, and Wheeler, to show he wasn't afraid of a dolphin, was about to take a header into the water when Nasmith called out, "Time's up! Next three in!" and that was the end of Wheeler's bathing for the day.

At 4.30 p.m. when all had had a turn, Nasmith himself last, they got under way again, the playful dolphin following. To let D'Oyly and Brown get their heads down, Nasmith took the first watch, from 8 p.m. till midnight. Instead of making for the signalling billet, he proceeded on various courses, working towards the centre of the Marmara far from the usual traffic routes, and charging the batteries. As the Turks knew, of course, that the submarine could only communicate with its base from the extreme western end of the Marmara, Nasmith decided to avoid it for the time being. He was now entirely of D'Oyly's opinion that the crew were not ready for fresh adventures. Besides, he didn't want to launch any more torpedoes until they had been thoroughly overhauled. The main object was to sink five more enemy ships with his five torpedoes: whether he did so on that day or a few days later was not of much importance. He decided to give the men as easy a time as possible on the following day. Except for the torpedomen, they could have a make and mend, and clean up the boat which was very foul.

When he was relieved at midnight, he went along to the wardroom, took his boots off and lay down on his bunk. The long green curtains were swaying gently with the movement of the boat. He closed his eyes, and still he could see them swaying. Suddenly he gave way to his fatigue. Great black waves rolled up and engulfed him: he didn't know whether they were waves of sleep or of the sea, he only knew that he was going down into oblivion, and he was past caring.

NINE

Nearly eight hours later, Nasmith became conscious again of the roar of the diesel engines and opened his eyes: they were dazzled by the glare of an electric bulb only a few feet away from him, so he closed them again. His throat felt dry, his head ached. The events of the previous day rushed back into his conscious mind, and gradually his eyes grew accustomed to the light, though they still smarted from hours of gazing through the periscope. He saw that Greene was laying the table for breakfast. It was the first time that he had slept for anything like as long as this, or as soundly, since the patrol started. He sat up and swung his legs over the edge of the bunk. Greene disappeared and returned with a cup of coffee. He sipped it and felt better.

D'Oyly came in with a cheerful "Good morning, Skipper!" and sat down to a plateful of eggs and bacon.

"What's the weather doing?" Nasmith asked.

"Clear and bright. Wind sou'west, force 2. We're about in the centre of the Marmara, heading due west and making a comfortable five knots."

"The batteries?"

"Densities 1240 and 1243. Temperatures 78 degrees and 80."

"That'll do. You can break the charge, and when the L.T.O.'s had his breakfast we'll look at the torpedoes. If you'll detail the men you need to handle them, the rest can clean up the boat. I wish we had some fresh water to spare for dhobeying – the place stinks like a charnel house."

"Could we use the fresh water in the barricoes we took out of the ammunition ship? I've been keeping it in reserve, but it might not be safe to drink it."

"Good idea. The cook had better start heating it up right away. But no dhobey lines on deck. A row of white sweaters fluttering in the breeze could be spotted miles away."

"O.K., Skipper. It's about time we boarded another ship – must replenish the larder, and I need some timber for my new raft."

D'Oyly hurried through his breakfast to go and issue the orders for the day's work and to relieve Brown who was on the bridge, while Nasmith got up and shaved. He couldn't help smiling about the raft, perhaps because Brown found it an endless source of amusement. Actually he didn't want to discourage D'Oyly's plan to swim ashore pushing a raft loaded with explosives to blow up the Baghdad Railway: it was perhaps a useful outlet for his boundless energy and imagination, and it had entertainment value for the men, which was also important. He decided to treat the plan more seriously in future.

When he had breakfasted, he went up to the bridge for a breath of air. They were lying stopped now on the surface and there was nothing in sight but the empty sea all round them, rippling and sparkling and lapping against the hull, and a bank of motionless fleecy clouds above the horizon to the east. The men were already busy with buckets of hot water and soap, washing their clothes for the first time in nine days. After a while D'Oyly came up and reported that one of the torpedoes was ready for inspection. He went below, climbed into his dungarees, and accompanied D'Oyly forward.

Of the five remaining torpedoes, three were invisible behind the polished brass doors of the stern and beam tubes; one was clamped to the side of the boat with the nose pointing forward in such a position that it could be loaded into the port bow tube with as little effort as possible: it was a shining steel cylinder, nearly seventeen feet from nose to tail, eighteen inches in diameter and weighing more than half a ton. The other was lying in sections on the battery boards with the L.T.O. kneeling beside it, and Clark, the fore-end man, who was responsible for the torpedo room, hovering anxiously behind him with a piece of oily waste in his hand.

In each torpedo there were six main chambers, any one of which could be detached for purposes of examination and adjustment. Nasmith was not concerned at the moment with the foremost chamber, which contained the explosive charge of 320 lb. of Trotyl, or with the second in which the compressed air was stored which supplied the motive power for the engines, but with the third, known as the balance chamber. It contained a pendulum weight attached to two rods which were connected up to the horizontal rudders. When the nose of the torpedo in Constantinople Harbour rose, the pendulum should have swung backward, deflecting the horizontal rudders downwards, and preventing it from jumping out of the water. They therefore tilted the balance chamber forwards and backwards to make sure that the pendulum weight was working properly, tested the connections to the rudders and also tested the small servomotor which was designed to assist its action.

The fourth chamber contained the Brotherhood three-cylinder engines which drove the torpedo forward at a speed of forty knots, together with the depth gear which controlled the depth at which it should run and could be fixed for anything from two feet to thirty. In this diminutive engine-room there was also a gyroscope, and it was to this that Nasmith paid particular attention. Its job was to keep the torpedo on a straight course, and the gyroscope of the torpedo that ran wild should

103

have prevented it from rushing off to one side and circling the harbour. Obviously it hadn't been set properly or it had got displaced. Nasmith and D'Oyly with all their expert knowledge were not able to decide exactly what had gone wrong with it, but they suspected that the tail plug had stayed in too long – this was a home-made affair, a plug in the exhaust pipe, devised by D'Oyly to prevent the water leaking into the engine while the torpedo was lying in the flooded tube. Of course, if it didn't pop out as soon as the torpedo was launched and the pressure of compressed air built up against it, the engine wouldn't start at once, and that might account for its erratic behaviour. All they could do was to make reasonably certain that it wouldn't happen again. At last, after exhaustive tests, Nasmith said he was satisfied.

"I don't think we'll have any trouble with this one," D'Oyly said.

"I've been thinking," Nasmith replied, "that we might have a little trouble with the sinking valve, accidentally on purpose, if you see what I mean." Although the engine-room was only thirty inches long, it contained, among a mass of delicate machinery, the range wheels and sinking valve which worked in conjunction, so that at the end of its run, in the event of a miss, water would pour into the torpedo's air and buoyancy chambers and send it to the bottom out of harm's way, "I'm doing this on my own responsibility," he went on, "but you needn't spread it around ..." and he set the range wheel so that the torpedo would float. "I want all the torpedoes set to float from now on, understand? We can't afford to lose a single one of them. If we miss, we'll pick it up again." The others nodded. It wasn't necessary to explain any further. "We'll take a look at the tail while we're about it," he said.

The fifth, or buoyancy chamber, also contained only compressed air like the second, but the hollow tail contained intricate connecting rods, gears and levers, allowing the pendulum weight and the servomotor to operate the horizontal rudders, and the engines to drive two four-bladed propellers revolving in opposite directions and each with a different pitch. On its outer surface, besides the propellers set close together, there were four pairs of vertical and horizontal rudders.

Half an hour later, Nasmith finally completed his inspection. He went back to the wardroom while the torpedo was being reassembled, and a working party under D'Oyly's supervision manhandled it into the starboard bow tube so that it was ready for use. He wasn't unduly worried about his action in setting his torpedoes to float although there was an international convention which said they must be set to sink, as otherwise they would be like floating mines, dangerous to friend and foe alike. He had no friends in the Marmara, and anyway, he intended to pick his torpedoes up again if he missed, so they wouldn't be a danger to anybody as floating mines. Besides, it was believed at that time that the Turks were using floating mines in the Dardanelles Straits, letting them drift down with the current among the blockading ships. Experts ascribed the loss of the battleships *Ocean, Irresistible* and *Bouvet* to these floating mines, and Keyes had warned his submarine commanders to be on the lookout for Turkish mine-dropping cruisers and torpedo them if possible.

When Nasmith and D'Oyly had completed their examination of the second torpedo, and the men had loaded it into the port bow tube, it was getting on for dinner time. Nasmith would have liked to tackle the other three, but as the object of hiding out in the centre of the Marmara for the whole day was to give everybody a rest, he agreed to D'Oyly's suggestion of a make and mend. That meant that only essential duties would be performed, and most of the men would be free to do what they pleased for the afternoon.

Nasmith felt that there was a general desire on the part of everybody, and particularly D'Oyly, to make it a day of celebration for the successful attack on Constantinople. Judging by the numbers of volunteers helping the cook, and the succulent smell being wafted through the boat, there was some special effort being made to produce a hot dinner instead of the usual cold bully beef and biscuits. When the tins of bully beef were opened, the fat was carefully scraped off the chunks of meat; ship's biscuits were hammered until they were reduced to powder, and the two were mixed together to make a kind of pastry that was rolled out on a board, an empty bottle being used as a rolling pin. The bully beef was stirred up in a pot with the contents of a tin of Yorkshire Relish – and somehow or other the combined efforts of the half-dozen volunteer cooks produced individual pies, baked in the electric oven, for every man on board.

The most popular order after dinner was naturally "Hands to bathe!" as the day was shimmering with heat, and the air that was drawn into the boat was too hot for comfort. D'Oyly and two of the men were busy constructing a mysterious contraption out of the loom of an oar and some boards – all that remained of

105

the things he had collected for his raft when they boarded the sailing vessel. It soon became apparent what it was.

"D'Oyly's made us a new periscope," Brown told Nasmith who came over to look at it. The loom of the oar was so balanced and weighted that it floated upright and protruded about two feet out of the water. Part of an old tobacco tin gave the effect of a hooded lens.

"You get the idea?" said D'Oyly.

"Sure," Brown replied. "It's a target, to give the Turks some practice in hitting periscopes – to help them to improve their aim."

"Well – more or less. Only they're meant to ram this one with a destroyer, and while they're ramming it ... tell me, what would you do?"

Brown thought for a moment. "I don't know ... I suppose I'd stand watching them, laughing like a drain."

"Yes, I suppose you would – but I'd torpedo them!"

Suddenly Dowell's clear voice rang out, "Aircraft bearing Green Two-O!"

"Diving stations!" roared Nasmith, and there was a rush of splashing, naked men to get back to the boat. D'Oyly leapt down the fore hatch, and in a few moments shouted back, "Shut off for diving!" while Dowell made for the hydroplane wheels. The tail clutches, connecting up the electric motors with the propellers, had been left in to be ready for an emergency. The plane could be heard now. Nasmith picked it up with his binoculars. "Good for Dowell!" he said. "We can laugh at this one. Flood the auxiliary! Ahead both. Take her down to thirty feet." He nodded to Brown to go below, then waved his cap derisively at the approaching plane, as if to say, "You haven't got a hope of hitting us, old boy," then he got down too, and closed the lid just before the water rushed over it. He had very little respect for the ability of airmen to hit their targets, but the ensuing Bang! was uncomfortably close. He waited while two more bombs burst in the water, then: "That's all right. He's dropped his load now. We'll go up again," and he brought E 11 to the surface. "Hands to bathe!" he shouted cheerfully as soon as he opened the hatch – but none of the men felt like it. He looked carefully all round with his binoculars. The aeroplane had gone – but he got quite a shock on seeing a periscope about a quarter of a mile away from them. Then he remembered it was D'Oyly's.

"You see?" D'Oyly said excitedly. "He must have aimed at

106

my wooden periscope! That's probably why he missed us!".

"That's probably why he damned nearly hit us, you mean," said Brown.

Anyway, Nasmith decided to go and pick it up. "Port ten," he ordered the helmsman, then, "Steady on Lieutenant D'Oyly-Hughes' periscope."

It was Nasmith's invariable practice to leave the area at once whenever he had been spotted, so, after picking up the periscope, he headed west for the signalling billet.

In the gathering dusk they reached the western end of the Sea of Marmara. There was just enough light remaining for them to get their bearings to establish their position. Finding that they were within thirty miles of *Jed*'s position keeping W/T watch for them on the other side of the Isthmus of Bulair, they stopped, raised the wireless masts and sent out their call sign. Leaving Brown on watch on the bridge, and two look-outs with night glasses, Nasmith went below. The night was dark and overcast. It was the most heavily patrolled area, because shipping from all parts of the Marmara converged there to enter the Straits of Gallipoli, but it would be impossible in the darkness to attack any ship that passed, however close it came to them, and there was the ever-present danger of being rammed by a destroyer, or even by a merchantmen that would be an easy victim in the daylight.

In the wardroom, when Nasmith joined him, D'Oyly was studying a map of the enemy's rail communications to the battle area. Both were conscious of the rapid high-pitched buzz of their little 11½ lb. transmitter that was sending the report of their achievements to the outer world. It was very long, for it described the sinking by demolition charge of the ammunition ship *Nagara*, the torpedoing of the second ammunition ship alongside the pier at Rodosto, the ship laden with barbed wire driven ashore – and finally the dramatic ending, "Dived into Constantinople Harbour and torpedoed a ship alongside the quay at Topkhana Arsenal." It was written as a routine report of a routine patrol, but they knew it would make the headlines all over the world – perhaps make history. It was more important, however, to Nasmith that he had at last justified the confidence that Roger Keyes always had in him all through the troubled and difficult days of the North Sea patrols since the beginning of the war. He could imagine the delight with which Keyes would read his signal, and how he would wave it under the nose of the Commander-in-Chief, and have it relayed immediately to the Admiralty. It might even strengthen his hand in his campaign for a more energetic policy, for Keyes embodied the Churchill spirit of fearless aggression. It was one of the tragedies of history, sensed by many officers serving at the time, that he occupied a subordinate position among the commanders of the forces in the Aegean roughly parallel to that of Churchill himself in London.

An hour passed ... two hours ... three hours ... and the thin pinging went on. Evidently Lohden was still having trouble with the set. The wind was rising, and the sea could be plainly heard lapping against the hull. Nasmith grew impatient, and went up to the bridge to join Brown. The sky was clearing. Stars were visible now among broken clouds, and a bright glow behind the line of the hills showed that the moon would soon appear. The aerial was sparking very badly, showing up the boat and the men's pale staring faces in a ghostly flickering light, dazzling the look-outs. He sent Brown down to the wireless cabin to see how Lohden was getting on, and he paced up and down the diminutive bridge. How dramatic, how ironic, it would be if they were surprised on the surface while their eyes were blinded by the transmission of the signal announcing their success! Brown returned and reported that the signal had been passed, and Lohden was about to receive one from *Jed*.

"It will keep till next time," Nasmith said. "Down wireless masts. Diving stations!" He sounded the klaxon. "Full ahead together on the motors." The orders were repeated, and E 11 glided forward. The time was 1.30 a.m. "Steer eighty-five degrees." He sent the helmsman below, but kept Brown and a look-out on the bridge.

"Shut off for diving," D'Oyly reported from below. They slipped almost noiselessly through the water, moving in an easterly direction. They were using the electric motors, and all the ventilators and exhaust vents were already closed so that they could dive quickly if necessary. The moon tipped the ridge of mountains and sent a silver stream of light across the sea.

The look-out raised his head suddenly: "Red Two O. Something moving, sir!"

Before Nasmith could focus his glasses on to it, Brown shouted, "Ship right ahead, sir." The moon went behind a cloud, and they lost sight of it again.

"Time 1.40," muttered Brown, scribbling in his notebook.

"Port thirty." Nasmith ordered down the voice-pipe to the

helmsman in the steering position in the control room. The boat swung round, and he steadied her only when they had turned a complete semi-circle and were following their own wake back the way they had come. He increased speed to keep ahead of the moving shapes until he could discern exactly what they were. Then: "Flood main ballast." The boat gradually lost buoyancy. He stopped flooding when her superstructure was awash, and only the conning tower and bridge were above water.

"Six feet on the depth-gauge, sir," Dowell reported, and the vents were closed so that no more water would enter the tanks. "Horizontal, sir!" came from below.

"Very good," Nasmith answered. "Send Mr. D'Oyly-Hughes to the bridge, please."

E 11 was now so low in the water that it would be very difficult for an enemy to see her. The moving shapes were gradually overhauling them. The three officers studied them through their night glasses: the two nearest were evidently destroyers, but between them, and farther away, there was a much larger ship – probably a store ship that they were escorting. None of them were showing lights. Brown noted their descriptions and their bearing, and estimated their course and speed. The ship loomed larger and larger and, as she crossed a patch of moonlit sea they made out, quite clearly, that she was a battleship.

"She's the *Barbarossa*!" said Nasmith. "She's giving us another chance!"

The attack was going to be a tricky thing to manage. It would have to be made on the surface, and without the use of his graded sights, because practically nothing can be seen through the periscope by moonlight. "If we submerge and come up again," he said, "when the destroyers have passed, we'll probably lose her. She's travelling too fast for us to catch up again if we once get astern of her – about twelve knots I should say. We'll have to let them overtake us, and hope to get close enough to hit the *Barbarossa* before we're spotted. See that everybody's on their toes, D'Oyly, particularly the men on the motor switchboards. I shall want full fields as I approach her, then an increase of speed to steady us on the target, and full fields again. I'll need Brown up here. Put the L.T.O. on the firing gear, and Plowman to the wheel. Flood bow tubes."

"Ay, ay, sir." And D'Oyly went below.

"Port ten," ordered Nasmith, then, "Steady!" From being directly in *Barbarossa*'s track, he was edging in towards the shore, hoping to get between her and the destroyer to starboard of her. He chose the landward side, thinking that he would be less visible against the land than to seaward. When he was satisfied with his position, he slowed down to reduce his wake, and to let the ships overtake him. The report came up from D'Oyly, "Bow tubes ready, sir." Brown was giving him at intervals the bearing and estimated speed of the target and their own course and speed, and the deflection that would have to be allowed. "What water have we got?" Nasmith asked him.

"Forty-five fathoms, sir."

They were almost abreast of the destroyer which had just started to zig-zag away from them. "I'm going to turn in towards the target now. You keep your eyes glued on that destroyer, and tell me if she alters course." He sent the look-out below, and went to the voice-pipe, "Group up! Full power! Starboard ten . . . Steady. Keep her steady now!" In one minute he would be in position to launch his torpedo. "Full fields! Stand by now . . ."

"Destroyer swinging, sir!" Brown sang out. "Destroyer altering towards. Heading straight for us, sir! Three hundred yards . . . Two hundred yards . . ."

"Get below!" Nasmith shouted, and sounded the klaxon. "Group up! Full ahead both! Fifty feet! Take her down quick!"

He had a glimpse of the sharp bows of the destroyer cutting through the sea, and the spray shooting out on each side of them, and he leapt down the hatch after Brown, pulling the lid shut and securing it after him. E 11 slid forward and down in a long oblique dive. In the control room they listened to the beat of the propellers growing louder and louder till they thundered overhead with the sound of a giant threshing-machine as the hands of the depth-gauge registered thirty feet.

"Steady her at fifty feet." Nasmith said calmly. "Close bow caps, and drain tubes. *Barbarossa* has got away again."

A few minutes later D'Oyly came aft to the control room. "Bad luck, sir," he said. "Must have been a near thing."

"Yes. I was about to fire when she came for us. I needed only one more minute." He felt the disappointment keenly, but didn't show it. "Never mind," he went on, "we'll meet her again! I've got *Barbarossa* written on one of these tin fish, and I'm going to see that she gets it!" This was a bit of bravado, he realised as soon as he had said it, to keep the men cheerful. It had come out quite spontaneously because he sensed that they

110

needed reassuring. He was thankful afterwards that he hadn't let himself in for something more serious, such as not smoking or drinking until he got her.

He thought it unlikely that one of the destroyers would be detached to hunt for a submarine in the moonlight, but he didn't want to take any chances. He remained submerged for the rest of the short summer night.

When they surfaced, the sun was already glinting on the white peaks of Marmara Island, and there were no ships in sight. Nasmith, leaving D'Oyly on watch, went below and turned in. They patrolled slowly to eastward, charging the batteries, and keeping well clear of the land after passing Marmara Island. While the torpedomen prepared the next torpedo for inspection – the one in the port beam tube – the rest of the men were set to work washing and cleaning the boat.

There was none of the feeling of a let-down such as they had experienced after failing to get the *Barbarossa* and *Turgut Reiss* on the first day of the patrol in the Narrows. Nasmith noticed that this time D'Oyly, speaking quite naturally, had said, "Bad luck, sir." It was not an expression he would have used earlier in the patrol. Because of his notorious bad luck, the subject was never mentioned, and even the word "luck" was avoided. Now everything was changed. The attack on Constantinople had at least done this for the crew – it had induced in them a feeling of absolute confidence. Their skipper was now not only respected and admired – he was lucky.

During the forenoon, when Brown was on watch, D'Oyly worked on the torpedoes – it was properly his responsibility and Nasmith left it all to him now. Each was drawn in turn from its tube, overhauled, tested chamber by chamber, and manhandled into its tube again. Then the firing mechanism was tested. By the end of the day, Nasmith felt that everything possible had been done to prevent another mechanical breakdown. Whether the five remaining torpedoes would find their targets or not would depend now upon his skill and judgment in attack.

Nothing was sighted all that day until at 5 p.m. a small steamer was reported. They broke the charge and went after her on the surface as she wasn't worth a torpedo. She had fine lines like a yacht, and did not appear to be deeply laden, or to be unduly alarmed by the approach of the submarine. She came towards them at a fair speed, and opened fire with a small gun. The shell burst in the sea about a hundred yards short.

"Diving stations! Trim for diving!" Nasmith sounded the

klaxons and told the helmsman and look-out to get inside. "Flood the auxiliary!"

Down below, men ran to close the ventilators, to pull the levers opening the Kingston valves that let the seawater flood into the ballast tanks and open the vents, to stand by the hydroplane wheels, while in the engine-room the E.R.A.s shut down the diesels and connected the clutch for the electric motors. The duty stoker struggled to close the great engine exhaust vent: Jupp, the chief E.R.A. ran to help him, and lent his great strength to the task, but it seemed like hours.

"When are those bloody engines going to be ready?" D'Oyly shouted.

"When you bloody well keep out of it!" Jupp gasped, completely losing his temper. A few seconds later, the vent was closed.

"Shut off for diving!" D'Oyly reported.

The yacht fired again: the round again fell short. Nasmith noted that the shooting was good for line, but bad for distance. "Full ahead together," he ordered. "Take her down to thirty feet." He came down and closed the lid. E 11 settled low in the water, dipped her bows and slid easily down to thirty feet. There was no longer any danger, but, for the first time, tempers had been seriously ruffled. Nasmith couldn't overlook Jupp's abusive and insubordinate language. He was put on the defaulter's list.

It seemed that the yacht was a Q Ship – a ship specially fitted out to act as a decoy for submarines – the last thing Nasmith had expected to meet in the Sea of Marmara. Either that, or the Turks were equipping all their steamers with guns – a desperate measure, as they urgently needed guns at Gallipoli. It would mean that their smaller ships, those not worth the expenditure of a torpedo, would be absolutely immune from attack until the British submarines were also equipped with guns and could shoot it out with them.

They now turned back to the signalling billet, because they had broken off contact with *Jed* rather unceremoniously the night before. Their set was so inefficient, it took so long to pass their signals – Brown reckoned only four words an hour, but it wasn't quite as bad as that – that Nasmith decided as a general policy to make contact more frequently and for shorter periods. This time they had only to report the unsuccessful attack on the *Barbarossa* and the Q Ship, and to ask if their new periscope top was going to be flown out to them. They were aware also

The Turkish railway system

that *Jed* was anxious to pass signals to them. They surfaced as soon as it was dark, and sent out their call sign.

While the signalling "exercise," as Brown called it, was going on, Nasmith sat in the wardroom drawing diagrams of the night attack on *Barbarossa*, Brown supplying from his notebook the times, courses and speeds of the ships. After exhaustive analysis, Nasmith came to the conclusion that he had acted correctly, and that his manœuvre had in fact given them the best chance to sink her. There had always been the risk that an exceptionally alert enemy look-out would spot them, and that was no doubt what happened. Although the night was full of shadows, they must have been shown up by the moon at the crucial moment – unless, of course, the destroyer hadn't seen them at all: it was quite possible that she altered course towards them quite by accident.

The only alternative to a close attack would have been to remain at a safe distance from the convoy, and loose off a couple of torpedoes at extreme range on the off chance of scoring a hit. This he had not felt justified in doing. Most probably he would have missed, and lost the torpedoes. Even set to float they would have been very difficult to find.

Later he went through every move again with D'Oyly so that he would gain as much experience as possible although his duties kept him below during an attack.

The signals from *Jed,* when at last they came through and Brown had decoded them, contained surprising reports from neutral sources of the confusion they had caused by their attack on Constantinople. The ship they torpedoed was *Stamboul* which sank in the harbour at Harem Iskelessi with upperworks still visible. The other torpedo struck Customs House Quay. The explosions, and the heavy gunfire from the batteries at Kassim Pasha and on the hills above St. Sophia, caused a panic among the population who thought that the Allied Fleet had arrived. Shops were closed, and there was a rumour that the Sultan and his Ministers would move across to Asia. Troops embarking in four transports were disembarked and did not sail.

A signal from the Commander-in-Chief suggested that enemy troop reinforcements, guns and ammunition would now be sent from Constantinople by train via Smyrna to Panderma to shorten the sea passage to Gallipoli, or to Uzun Keupri and thence by road. Also that troops and supplies from Syria might be shipped direct from Ismid to Gallipoli.

It was a great satisfaction to Nasmith to learn that his second torpedo had run true, and *Stamboul* had sunk. It made the attempt a serious stroke of war, and not merely a propaganda demonstration. As Harem Iskelessi was over on the Asiatic side of the Bosphorus opposite the arsenal, the Turks had evidently towed *Stamboul* away from the quay where she was sinking, and tried to beach her where she wouldn't obstruct the traffic of the port.

He traced out with D'Oyly the probable course of the fugitive torpedo, ending at the Customs House Quay at Galata. It seemed extraordinary that it hadn't struck one of the anchored ships in its mad rush round the harbour. The stories of panic and the possible transfer of the Government he thought greatly exaggerated, so he paid little attention to them, except to note for future reference the positions of the various batteries mentioned.

The signal from the Commander-in-Chief was of far greater importance. He took it as an order to proceed first to Panderma on the southern coast, due south of Rodosto, and then to Ismid at the extreme eastern end of the Marmara.

In the final signal passed by *Jed*, it was regretted that no new periscope top was available – so Nasmith would have to make do with the other one for the remainder of the patrol.

TEN

At 1 a.m. on Friday the 28th of May, they broke off W/T contact with *Jed* and headed eastward on the surface. This time they sighted nothing during the night, but at 6 a.m. Brown, who was on watch, called down the voice-pipe extension to Nasmith that several patches of smoke had been sighted on the horizon to the north-east. He immediately went up to the bridge.

By 6.30 it could be seen that the smoke was caused by five merchant vessels escorted by a destroyer that was zig-zagging ahead of them. Having fixed their relative positions and estimated their course and speed, Nasmith ordered "Diving stations" and went down to thirty feet, long before there was any danger of them sighting him. He got into position ahead of the convoy and waited for it to approach, taking a look at the ships through the periscope at regular intervals, and allowing Brown and D'Oyly to do the same.

The convoy consisted of one large ship and four smaller ones. At 7.15 he dived under the destroyer which passed over him suspecting nothing. He rose to twenty feet and, moving very slowly to cause no feather of spray when he raised the periscope, and to leave no wake, he edged into position to attack the large ship. At 7.30 he fired the port bow tube. The torpedo struck the large ship on the port side aft, making a very loud report that nearly frightened Brown out of his skin as he had dozed off over the chart table during the attack.

As the destroyer was at some distance from them, Nasmith watched the effect of his shot. On the impact of the torpedo there was a huge column of smoke and flames, and the stricken vessel seemed to be lifted out of the water aft. Then she settled down, heeled over to starboard and sank in less than a minute after being hit, leaving only some floating debris. The smaller ships continued steadily on their course, but the destroyer turned, made for the position of the submarine and evidently sighting the periscope, or estimating its whereabouts from the direction of the track made by the torpedo, opened fire with her forward guns. Nasmith ordered "Down periscope" and "Dive to eighty feet."

E 11 went down in a long dive and straightened out. "Seventy feet, sir," the coxswain reported after a pause.

"The order was eighty feet."

"Can't get her down any lower, sir."

Nasmith was immediately on the alert. He watched the depth-gauge intently. The coxswains were bringing her up a few feet to try again. It registered sixty-five feet, then sixty feet, then the bows dipped as they worked the hydroplanes to bring her down at a steeper angle. If his half-perceived theory was correct, this would have no effect. Again she stuck at seventy feet. He could see that the coxswains were puzzled and uneasy, and he didn't want to try any experiments that might upset the trim when there was a destroyer hunting for them overhead.

"Hydroplane wheels back to the zero mark," he snapped. The coxswains mechanically obeyed. The boat remained under control and levelled off at seventy feet. "Keep her at seventy feet." He told Brown to mark their position on the chart. He had gained another scrap of knowledge that might help him to solve the problem of the lost submarines.

He continued diving until he considered that he had reached a safe distance, then called for silence. Everyone listened: there was no sound except the hum of the electric motors. He rose to thirty feet, and ordered, "Up periscope." The destroyer was still hunting vigorously for them in the wake of the convoy – which meant he couldn't surface and follow the other ships. His underwater speed was insufficient to overtake them, and so he had no alternative but to break off the action and let them escape. When the destroyer was out of sight, he surfaced and continued his patrol. This was a routine attack, faultlessly carried out, and it left him with four unexpended torpedoes.

From the size and position of the convoy, he thought that it must have come from Constantinople, the principal source of supplies, but there was nothing to prove it. The signals relayed to him by *Jed* seemed to imply that all traffic had ceased from there, and that the port was virtually closed: but of course the British authorities could only study and appraise the various

116

reports from neutral or secret sources and deduce from them the probable actions of the enemy. He alone, being on the spot, could find out what was really going on. At 11.30 he stopped on the surface in a position near Oxia Island from which he could observe the approaches to Constantinople.

The day was very warm, and a heat haze was beginning to reduce visibility when, at noon, a ship was observed leaving the harbour and shaping course towards Panderma. She was a fair-sized ship, certainly worth a torpedo, and she looked an easy victim.

"That's an unlucky ship," said Brown observing her. "She shouldn't have sailed on a Friday."

At 12.30 E 11 dived and began stalking her. When they got nearer, Nasmith could see through the periscope that her decks were crowded, so it seemed that troops were already being transported again, only three days after his attack on the harbour, and they were not even being escorted by destroyers. He was disappointed that the reports he had received had so greatly exaggerated the demoralising effect of the torpedoing of *Stamboul* – but on the other hand, if the sea route from Constantinople to Gallipoli was still being used by enemy troopships, there would be plenty of targets.

His face was unusually grim as he manœuvred into the attacking position, for it is not a light thing to loose wholesale death and destruction on an unsuspecting enemy ship, particularly when you can see people moving about on her decks who will soon be struggling in the water, but he was thinking also of what a shipload of Turkish soldiers were going to do on the battlefields of Gallipoli.

At 1.45 he closed to a thousand yards and fired the starboard beam tube. He watched the track running straight for the ship, estimating that she would be struck under the bridge. Brown stood, watch in hand, waiting to time the run of the torpedo. They heard no explosion – but the ship stopped. What had happened? Nasmith hesitated. Was she damaged? Should he expend another torpedo? But if it was a miss, why had she stopped? The smoke from her single funnel curled straight up into the blue sky, and she let off steam in a small white cloud. After a few minutes she went on again on a course that would bring her closer to E 11. Still Nasmith hesitated, his eyes glued to the lens, and did nothing. All at once he raised his head and looked strangely at Wheeler who was standing beside him. "She's not a troopship," he said. "Take a look, Wheeler."

Wheeler looked through the periscope and saw that the decks of the ship were crowded with civilians, including women and children. "What luck, sir, that you missed."

"Luck's not the right word for it," Nasmith said. "Down periscope."

To avoid being sighted and reported, he waited for the ship to get well clear. D'Oyly came aft and asked what was the matter.

"Apparently the story about the panic wasn't exaggerated after all. They're evacuating civilian women and children, so we can be thankful she didn't go up. But that doesn't alter the fact that the setting of the torpedo was incorrect. There was nothing wrong with my aim, I'm certain of it. Either it was a dud, or you didn't have the correct depth setting."

"Baker!" D'Oyly shouted.

"Yessir?"

"What did you set it to run at?"

"Ten feet, sir."

"Sure?"

"Yessir!"

"And I checked it," said D'Oyly. "If it ran deep, it was defective."

"Well, we'll soon find out. Take over, D'Oyly," said Nasmith abruptly, "and let me know when the ship's out of sight. Stay in the area, but don't go any nearer the torpedo." He went by himself to the wardroom. He heard some of the crew abusing the torpedomen, and Dowell's voice shutting them up, then he lay down on his bunk, his mind full of the horror that might have happened – and somehow didn't.

When the ship had gone, they surfaced and cruised around until they found their torpedo bobbing up and down in the sea. They stopped some distance away, in case it should go up on the firing pistol being touched, and damage the submarine. As they didn't carry a small boat, Nasmith stripped off his sweater, shoes and trousers, and dived into the sea. He came back to the side of the boat, called for a spanner which he hung round his neck, and swam to the torpedo. He saw at once that it had struck the ship, for the top of the head was crushed in, but for some reason it had failed to explode.

Before a torpedo is fired, and for about the first forty-five yards of its run, it is "safe," and could not be detonated with a hammer, but the "Whiskers," small propeller blades on its nose, begin to revolve as it passes through the water. These are fitted to a sleeve which is threaded for half its length, and then plain. When the whiskers have worked down the thread and reached the plain part, it means that the firing pin is barely one sixteenth of an inch away from the fulminate of mercury in the detonator. Nasmith saw that this stage had been reached on his torpedo and that a tap would cause it to explode. With infinite care he unscrewed the firing pistol containing the whiskers, the firing pin, the fulminate of mercury and the small charge of guncotton that would detonate the main charge, drew it out of the nose of the torpedo and set it to "safe." Then he moved along the side of the torpedo until he could reach the starting lever and push it forward in case, if some compressed air was left in the engine, the propellers should start revolving again and perhaps injure one of the crew. He swam back to the boat bringing the firing pistol with him. In the meantime the derrick over the forehatch, specially placed to handle torpedoes, had been rigged: it was kept in the casing and only had to be lifted up and fitted into a socket in the deck.

It took careful manœuvring now to lay the submarine alongside the seventeen-foot-long bobbing torpedo, to pass a sling under it at the point of balance and shackle a wire to it, to fit a nose line and a tale line to keep it from swinging, and hoist it on board. It was lowered on to the deck for the artificers to remove the warhead – the first chamber containing the explosive charge – because with it the torpedo would have been too long to bring in through the hatch. There was a pause while the three officers scanned the horizon with their binoculars, looking in every direction to make sure that no enemy was in sight, and listened for the sound of planes. Then Nasmith gave the order for the forehatch to be opened. This was the signal for intense activity, for every man knew that it would be impossible to dive, whatever the emergency, until it could be closed again. The forehatch was unclipped and thrown open in a moment, but it took several minutes to unbolt the strongbacks under it – curved steel girders to strengthen it, which continue the curve of the ribs. The torpedo was hoisted by a hand winch until it was suspended on the derrick over the open hatch, then it was tipped up and lowered gradually tail first into the interior of the submarine, with men below to guide it down. It was with immense relief that Nasmith saw the torpedo and the warhead disappear from view, and he could order the hatch to be closed and the strongbacks bolted into place again.

With Brown on watch, the patrol was continued while

Nasmith and D'Oyly examined the salvaged torpedo. First they opened the fourth chamber and looked at the depth gear – it was correctly set to run at a depth of ten feet, so the torpedomen were exonerated. It was looked upon as something of a miracle that the torpedo had actually struck the ship and not exploded. Nasmith's opinion was that it had run deep, struck the ship's side very low down and passed on beneath it, so that the firing pistol projecting from the nose had not made contact. That was the most satisfactory explanation they could arrive at, though they still marvelled that the shock of the concussion against the ship's side hadn't been sufficient to detonate it, and there were many arguments and discussions about it in the mess decks, and in the wardroom also. Brown admitted that he had been entirely wrong – it hadn't been unlucky for that ship to sail on Friday after all. D'Oyly insisted that it was Nasmith's fault that the torpedo didn't explode – it was obviously the one with *Barbarossa* written on it.

"That's as good an explanation as any," Nasmith said.

The E.R.A.s had the job of hammering the phosphor-bronze casing of the warhead into shape again, after the L.T.O. had removed the 320 lb. charge of Trotyl, and the result of it all was that after some hours' work, Nasmith again had four useful torpedoes at his disposal. It was loaded into the starboard beam tube.

No other ships came out of Constantinople Harbour while they kept it under observation. At 4 p.m. Brown reported through the voice-pipe extension to the wardroom that he had sighted a sailing vessel. Nasmith went up to have a look at her. She didn't appear to have any deck cargo, or to be deeply laden, but he decided to examine her. They overhauled her at 4.30. She was very much smaller than the sailing vessel they boarded last – little more than a caique. She sat gracefully on the water, her bow and stern curled up like the toe of a Turkish shoe. She was painted green and white and had a single low mast with a very long spritsail boom, and saffron-coloured sails.

They ran alongside her, making signs to the Captain to down sails. He understood immediately, and complied. He shouted to his mate to take the line heaved by a seaman from E 11's bows. D'Oyly and three armed seamen jumped aboard.

While D'Oyly searched her, Nasmith cast off again, though she looked quite inoffensive, and waited at a distance. He was always expecting that the wily Turk would one day set a trap for him. The problem of the sailing vessels was always on his mind. There were hundreds of them, and each could carry a fair cargo of stores, perhaps fifty or a hundred tons, machine guns, shells or boxes of ammunition. Sooner or later, he felt sure, the Turks would use them instead of the vulnerable store ships. It seemed a much more practical idea than sending their supplies hundreds of miles by rail to be transhipped into merchantmen at Panderma for the shorter sea passage, during which he might still torpedo them, or into bullock wagons at Uzun Keupri. On the other hand he sympathised with the boatmen and didn't want to inflict loss or hardship on them if they were merely going about their peacetime occupations. For the present it was only necessary to search them. The first time he found one carrying war supplies, he would have to begin sinking them, burning them, or blowing them up, depending on the nature of their cargo. Perhaps ramming them would be the best way, certainly the quickest way, as the submarine's sharp bows could easily crash through their timbers – they all carried small boats, so there need be no loss of life – or he might burn them at night in full view of the coast towns and particularly of the capital: it would have a frightening effect. . . .

"Mr. D'Oyly-Hughes signalling, sir."

He ran up alongside again. D'Oyly had found no contraband, but he had collected the usual assortment of delicacies – chickens, eggs, butter, cigarettes, dried fruit and three large baskets of ripe cherries. Some odd bits of timber also, to build another raft. There was a woman on board, evidently the captain's wife, who was crying bitterly, but the captain, delighted to be left in possession of his life, his ship and most of his cargo, was only too happy to let them take all the provisions they could find.

So that evening they supped royally again, and were in high good humour. D'Oyly, however, was unusually silent. Nasmith was aware that something had upset him, and he was worried about it because he valued his friendship, and the smooth working of his command depended largely on the perfect understanding between them. When they were alone in the wardroom together, during the usual "signalling exercises" with *Jed*, it all came out.

"You know, Skipper," D'Oyly began solemnly, "you shouldn't have swum out and unscrewed the firing pistol."

The way he put it, it might have been a reproach because his captain had run an unnecessary risk, so Nasmith answered rather guardedly, "Oh, well, I knew that I could do it. I'd have been worried if one of the men had been trying it, knowing

121

that he might bungle it and lose the firing pistol or blow himself up."

"Torpedoes are my job," D'Oyly protested. It was clear now that his only objection was that Nasmith had robbed him of the honour. "You will allow me to do it next time?"

"All right. Certainly, if you wish," he answered casually and dismissed the subject. He had swum out to deal with the firing pistol simply because he considered himself to be the best man for the job, but he could understand how D'Oyly felt about it – it must be difficult for a man of his adventurous spirit to be always second in command, to be always in readiness to take over complete responsibility for the boat, and never doing so. He would have to be careful in future not to rob him of any opportunity to show his initiative.

D'Oyly, however, having made his point, thought no more about it. "We got that fish in pretty smartly, didn't we?" he went on. "Must have been a record."

"Yes," Nasmith agreed, "but still it won't do. If anything had come along while the forehatch was open, we wouldn't have been able to deal with the situation. I've been thinking ... as the torpedoes are launched out of the tubes, why shouldn't they come in again the same way?"

"Like the one in Constantinople nearly did? We don't want that again!"

"No, I don't mean like that exactly ... chuck us a signal pad, will you?" He began to work out his idea, sketching it at the same time. "It would have to come in head first ... after removing the firing pistol, of course ..."

"But how are we going to push it in?"

"Once the nose is in – that's the idea of bringing it in head first – if we pump out the tube, it would have to come wouldn't it? I mean, it would be sucked in."

"I suppose so." D'Oyly looked doubtful. "We can try, anyway."

"Then, let's see ... we've got the torpedo in the tube again. Close stern cap ... but it's in the tube the wrong way round – see? So we open the inner door, making sure all the water is drained out first, of course, and pull it into the boat."

"Couldn't you persuade it to come in tail first?"

"No. It wouldn't suck in by the tapering end, and we might damage the rudders. But it doesn't matter. Suppose we bring it in nose first through the stern tube, all we have to do is to bring it through the boat and push it into one of the bow tubes,

122

or swing it through ninety degrees over the beam tubes and use it there."

"Sounds too easy. There must be a catch in it. If it works, why wasn't it always done that way?"

"I don't know. We'll try it next time. The beauty of it is that we can dive at any time. The boat will never be in danger from open hatches."

They were still trying to find a possible snag when Lohden came in with a signal. D'Oyly went up to the bridge so that Brown could come down and decode it. It was not a very welcome signal, and it was also rather obscure, owing to difficulties with the reception. It contained a report that aerial reconnaissance – one of Commander Samson's planes, that is – had discovered enemy ships near the Marmara entrance to the Gallipoli Straits.

There was not much that Nasmith could do about it. If they were on passage when they were reported, they would obviously be no longer there. If they were hanging around, they might be small ferry boats transferring troops from the Asiatic to the European side of the Straits, perhaps from Chardak or Lampsaki Bay where a road from Panderma reaches the shores of the Straits. He wouldn't be able to attack them because of their shallow draft, and because they would be protected by the minefield.

Because the entrance to the Straits was nearly always guarded by enemy destroyers, Nasmith's policy had been to intercept ships before they got there, in the wider stretches of the Marmara that could not be always covered by patrols. However, at the signalling billet he was already near the entrance to the Straits, and he could not reasonably ignore the report that he was obviously intended to investigate. The charge was kept on until daylight. Then, at 4 a.m. they dived and turned west. It was a blustering and uninviting day with a choppy sea running and the sun obscured by heavy clouds, very unlike the golden days they had become accustomed to in the Marmara. The cliffs and hills on both sides looked sombre and monotonous.

At 7 a.m. they sighted a laden store ship coming from the east. They turned towards her and increased speed to head her off. There was little danger of the periscope being seen in the broken water. They got into the attacking position, and Nasmith waited confidently for the ship to come into his sights, but the boat unexpectedly dipped, and when he wanted to fire he could see nothing as the top of the periscope was underwater. "Hold her up!" he shouted, exasperated. "Twenty feet!" Steady her at twenty feet!" – but she went on down, and when the coxswains got her bows up again, she came right up and broke surface in full view of the steamer, which immediately altered course away. While the submarine lay on the surface, Nasmith and D'Oyly carefully adjusted her trim. They flooded her ballast tanks until she was awash, then, watching the spirit level to measure the angle of her dive, they took her down to twenty feet. This time she answered to her hydroplanes and remained perfectly under control, but the ship, fortunately an unarmed merchantman, presenting her stern to them, headed for the entrance to the Straits at her best speed and it was impossible to catch up with with her again.

While they patrolled up and down, waiting for another ship to appear, Nasmith dealt with the case of the defaulter, Jupp – the large Chief E.R.A. with the great black shaggy beard. Everybody was tired, and outbursts of temper and frayed nerves were to be expected, but this was a serious breach of discipline. It is against the regulations, and the tradition, of the Navy to answer an officer back, whatever the provocation. Jupp should have kept quiet when D'Oyly swore at him, but he would have been within his rights if he had lodged a complaint afterwards. The special problem here was that Jupp was a valuable man who could not be replaced. The way Nasmith settled the case was this: he degraded Jupp from chief E.R.A. to second, and promoted Brooker from second chief, instructing him to act under Jupp's advice and supervision. Thus he punished Jupp without depriving himself of his great experience and efficiency with the engines. All the chief petty officers during the time they were on patrol in the Marmara were paid as warrant officers, so the loss to Jupp was considerable.

They continued their patrol all day and sighted nothing worth attacking. In the afternoon, two destroyers appeared. One zig-zagged regularly from side to side off the entrance, while the other patrolled farther out into the Marmara.

D'Oyly came and asked permission to try out the decoy periscope. It was an ideal day for it: for a moment it would be visible, then lost, then seen again in the choppy sea. Nasmith agreed, more for the entertainment value than for anything else, as it was a boring patrol for the men. It worked like a charm. In no time the men were talking and laughing as they assembled the contraption and put the finishing touches to it.

124

When it was ready, they waited until the nearest destroyer had taken a wide sweep away from them, surfaced so that only the conning tower was above water, dragged the dummy periscope up the conning tower hatch and launched it into the sea. It looked remarkably life-like. They submerged again, drew discreetly away just keeping it in sight, and waited for something to happen. Soon the destroyer went about in leisurely fashion and moved towards them. Tension mounted in the submarine. She must have had excellent look-outs, for before Nasmith believed it possible, she increased to full speed, headed directly for the dummy and opened fire.

"Take the periscope, D'Oyly," he said. "It's your show."

D'Oyly seized the training handles and pressed his eyes to the lens. "She's taken the bait!" he shouted. "She's rushing straight towards it! Can we torpedo her, sir?"

"Not on your life! I'm not wasting a torpedo on a small fast-moving destroyer."

"One mile to go," D'Oyly went on. "Must be doing thirty knots! What a bow wave! Spray flying all over the place. Firing again now – shots falling round the dummy. Good shot, sir! Nearly got it! Coming in now to ram.... What a surprise she'll get when nothing happens. Two hundred yards now ... Turkish captain already sees himself being decorated by the sultan and being given the pick of the harem. Stand by for the crash! Now for it! zizzz! She's dashed right over it!" He roared with laughter, and so did the men. He stepped back from the periscope to let Nasmith have a look. "She's turning for another run, sir."

Once again the intrepid destroyer dashed for the decoy, and then at last realised that there was something peculiar about it. She dropped a boat and went on circling suspiciously.

"She's going to pick it up," said Nasmith at the periscope. "The other destroyer is coming nearer – I think it's time we moved off."

D'Oyly was thrilled with the success of his trick. "You see? It worked wonderfully! Next patrol we'll bring a mine and hang it on the base of the dummy."

"Oh, no, you don't!" Nasmith laughed. "We've nearly torpedoed ourselves already, we're not going to blow ourselves up with a mine as well. By the way – what was under it?"

"A weight, a long string, and a bottle."

"Empty bottle?"

"Brasso put a message in it. What did you write, Brasso, for the Turkish skipper?"

" ' 'Ave you ever been 'ad,' sir."

"They'll have a high old time translating that, won't they?"

ELEVEN

"The Marmara is reputed to be the sea of mirages," D'Oyly said after supper that evening in the wardroom. He seemed to be leading up to something, so Nasmith pushed aside his empty coffee cup and leant back comfortably to let him feel that this would be a good time to say whatever it was that he had on his mind. "I wish we knew," D'Oyly went on, "why the boat was heavy coming up the Straits, why we lost control at Constantinople, why she wouldn't go below seventy feet yesterday and why she wouldn't answer to the hydroplanes to-day. The men are saying that it must be the ghost again."

So that was it. Most of the men had been with him in E 11 one November afternoon in Heligoland Bight when something happened that he had never been able to explain; the sort of thing you tell yourself afterwards couldn't possibly have happened and perhaps you were over tired, your mind playing tricks out of sheer exhaustion – but this experience was shared by the whole ship's company. He had made an unsuccessful attack on three destroyers in line ahead when suddenly his bow was jerked up to a startling angle. He flooded the fore trimming tank to prevent her from breaking surface, but she showed no disposition to rise: she stayed at her original depth, taking angles by the bow and stern in defiance of the laws of hydrostatics, so he took her to the bottom in ninety feet and weighted her down with plenty of ballast. Then the noises started – not only the rushing of propellers, but other noises, indescribably weird, quite close overhead. After a while he rose to adjust the trim, but she again took an angle of twenty degrees by the bow, so he took her down again and held her to the bottom. He told the men to fall out from their diving stations, and while they had tea they listened to the curious noises overhead which continued for two whole hours. Abruptly they ceased. He took her off the bottom and found her in perfect trim and answering to the controls as if she had never given any trouble. He put up the periscope and found nothing in sight except Heligoland in the distance.

"No, D'Oyly, I don't think the ghost has followed us here," he said. "The coxswains simply made a mistake to-day, let her go down, then tried to correct the movement too quickly and let her come up. Perhaps we had an untidy trim, but we don't need to make a mystery of it. Coming up the Straits – that's another matter. I've got a theory about our difficulties there that might help also to explain the loss of E 15, AE 2, *Joule* and *Saphir*. Look, I'll show you . . ."

He sent for Brown, and together they went through the courses, speed and depth variations, compass bearings, and the orders he had given on the way up, which were recorded in Brown's notebook. The conclusion was inescapable: allowing for the manœuvres round Nagara Point, their average speed had been greater measured over the ground than through the water. Instead of having a current against them of from one to four knots, they had actually had a favourable current of one knot. The implications of this discovery were tremendous. It meant that heavy seawater was constantly flowing up into the Marmara, while the lighter fresh water, sliding over the top of it, was flowing down – like two rivers flowing in opposite directions one above the other. In the Straits, and probably over the whole of the Marmara, there was fresh water only near the surface. Ironically he had been given the clue to the secret right at the beginning – two clues – and hadn't recognised them. The first was contained in the old legend that C. G. Brodie had unearthed about the body of the superfluous member of the Sultan's household which had been put into a weighted sack and thrown into the sea, and later turned up again under the walls of the Seraglio: the second was in the curse of Xerxes when he called the waters salt – they were salt, thirty feet down.

As a result of his experiences in the estuaries of the German rivers, Nasmith was very well aware of the dangers of navigating in partly fresh and partly salt waters. To pass from one layer of density to another would be equivalent to removing, or adding, a twenty-ton weight – more than enough to make a delicately balanced submarine lose her trim. Probably there was a difference in density when E 11 refused to rise near Kephez, and when B 6 with Brodie on board would not submerge below forty feet and afterwards dived at an acute angle to ninety feet and levelled off for no apparent reason – she had got down to a layer of seawater. To deal with this problem they would have to keep most careful records and try to discover at what depths the different layers of density might be encountered, remembering that these again might be affected by bad weather or differences in temperature.

"But doesn't all the seawater get mixed with the fresh water in the Straits and get carried out again?" D'Oyly objected. "I mean, where does it go to? It must come out again somewhere."

"Of course it needs a more scientific investigation than we can manage, but I'm going to try an interesting experiment . . ."

When it grew dark, and they had sighted nothing, Nasmith turned eastward. Without stopping to communicate with *Jed*, as he had nothing to report, he made for the area in which they had had difficulty in diving beyond seventy feet. As soon as Brown reported that they had reached the position he had marked on the chart, he ordered diving stations, and repeated the previous day's manœuvre: he took E 11 down in a long gradual dive to seventy feet. Then he ordered eighty feet. Again the coxswain reported that she wouldn't go any lower. The boat was going ahead, the hydroplanes were hard down – but she wouldn't go down.

"Flood the auxiliary!" He let in three tons of seawater ballast. It had no effect. He let in three more, and then another three. Still she wouldn't go down. "All right," he said, "try coming up."

The coxswain put the hydroplanes hard up – but she wouldn't come up, as she was weighted down by nine tons of extra ballast.

Nasmith was thoroughly enjoying himself, because his experiment was a success, but the men were bewildered. "If you can't go down, and you can't come up, then stop everything," he said. The engines stopped. The boat gradually lost way. There was dead silence. "I want one man on watch, Dowell. He is to call me at once if the depth alters. Everyone else can turn in. Fall out diving stations." He strolled away to the wardroom, followed by D'Oyly and Brown.

It was the first time it had ever been heard of for a submarine to lie suspended in the water: they were still at a depth of seventy feet, and there were more than two hundred feet of water underneath them, between the keel and the sea bed. Instead of going at once to their quarters on being released from duty, the men hung about, talking uncertainly. However, as Nasmith was quite unconcerned, they quickly accepted the situation.

Nasmith's discovery was that, instead of there being a gradual, or even a fairly rapid change in density, as he had imagined it, there was a rigid line of demarcation. The layers slid over each other, usually moving in different directions, not mingling. The submarine, in the fresh-water layer, was now resting on the surface of the heavier salt-water layer as solidly as if she were on the bottom. This was perfectly safe, but in the Straits with the salt water thrusting up where the bottom shelved and getting mixed with the fresh water and forming pockets of heavier density, with the cross currents going in all directions, navigation for a submarine could be extremely dangerous.

Nasmith's trick of making use of this phenomenon solved some of his most urgent problems. The men were tired, and so was he. Even when they were off duty they had had to be ready to go to their diving stations at a moment's notice when the klaxons sounded. Now they could all be off duty for the whole night, except for one man watching the depth-gauge. There was complete silence and no enemy could disturb them. It was more secure than lying on the sea bed, for the few places in the Marmara where it was shallow enough to do so were usually patrolled, and the beat-beat-beat overhead of an enemy's propeller, particularly when it passed and repassed, was a strain on the nerves. The engines too had been overworked. They required maintenance and minor repairs which could only be done when they could be stopped for several hours. Now, whenever he judged that the men needed a rest, or the artificers wanted to tinker with the engines, he had only to take the boat to seventy feet and let it lie there for as long as necessary.

There was, of course, still the problem of the foulness of the air, an increasing problem, for the smell of their damp sweat-sodden clothing grew more and more oppressive. As the day following their first peaceful night at seventy feet was a Sunday, Nasmith took E 11 farther out into the centre of the Marmara and surfaced out of sight of land. The sky was still overcast, the sea uninviting, and only two or three of the crew were willing to take advantage of the first call of "Hands to bathe!" After prayers and Swedish Drill, Nasmith allowed the coxswain to issue a small amount per man of their precious fresh water for washing and dhobeying, and soon all hands were busy scrubbing their clothes, and sweeping and cleaning the boat. In the afternoon there was a make and mend – the men were left to their own devices, except for the look-outs and those on duty in the engine-room. Hymn tunes were played on the gramophone.

129

Nasmith noticed that D'Oyly's raft was taking shape again. It was constructed in such a way that it could be rapidly assembled and dismantled – he didn't mean to lose a second one. It was tried out and found to be capable of bearing the weight of a 14½ lb. demolition charge and firing pistol together with D'Oyly's clothes, revolver and specially sharpened bayonet. Then it was lifted out of the water, dismantled and stowed away until it should be wanted.

If the signal outlining the probable change in the enemy's use of supply routes was to be taken seriously, there was a stronger case than before for D'Oyly's projected raid on the railway. The fact that refugees – and not, apparently, troops – were being shipped from Constantinople, forced Nasmith to take that signal more seriously than he had at first intended. He was very unwilling to let D'Oyly risk his life in so desperate an enterprise but, on the other hand, he didn't want to oppose it unreasonably. It was a perfectly legitimate plan, and he knew that Keyes would approve of it. Their business was to attack the enemy, and to keep on attacking. The railway seemed to be a vulnerable point. It was clear that the blowing up of a section of the line, if he really succeeded in doing it, could only cause temporary delay in the traffic, but it would have a news and prestige value of the same kind as their raid on Constantinople Harbour. It might also induce the enemy to divert some manpower to guard exposed sections of the line, and perhaps place defensive guns at key points, all of which would help to dissipate his war effort.

After dinner in the wardroom they pulled out the map of the enemy system of rail communications and studied the Commander-in-Chief's signal in conjunction with it. It suggested that enemy troops, guns and ammunition would now be sent from Constantinople by train via Smyrna to Panderma to shorten the sea passage to Gallipoli. They traced the route on the map. The trains would be loaded at the Haidar Pasha terminus at Scutari on the Asiatic side of the Bosphorus. The railway makes a long detour, south, west, then north again, a distance of about 640 miles to Panderma which is only seventy miles from Constantinople by sea. There everything would have to be trans-shipped into steamers, which still might be torpedoed. The first section of the railway runs along the coast for about thirty miles in the Gulf of Ismid, and it was there that D'Oyly planned to strike.

If the enemy, instead of pouring shiploads of men and material by the sea route into Gallipoli were really being forced to load them into trains for a long detour, it would mean that Nasmith's operations had been more successful than he had ever dreamed they could be. The difficulties and delays would be considerable, and about a dozen freight trains would be required to carry as much as a single ship of five thousand tons. There was one other route they could use to the north of the Sea of Marmara entailing a train journey of 150 miles to Uzun Keupri near the Bulgarian frontier. There was a road to Gallipoli from there, and a system of transport by bullock wagon which took about five days, and the last part of the road, along the Bulair Isthmus, off which *Jed* was keeping watch, was exposed to the fire of the British naval guns. There were only two possible routes for heavy material or supplies in bulk – by sea from Constantinople to Gallipoli, and by sea from Panderma to Gallipoli – and E 11 threatened both of them.

The shortest route from Panderma to Gallipoli was through a channel three miles wide between the southern shores of Marmara Island and Artaki Peninsula. At 8 p.m. of that Sunday evening, E 11 took up station at the eastern end of this channel. The weather had cleared, and in the soft starlight they could make out the rugged contours of the hills, and below them white villages and dark patches of shadow both on Artaki Peninsula and on Marmara Island. It would not have been easy for anyone to distinguish them against the background of the land, but they would easily sight a ship approaching from the direction of Panderma. They lay on the surface, trimmed well down, and used the motors only occasionally to counteract the effect of the strong current which otherwise would have swept them to westward into the Marmara Channel. They kept watch all night, but no ships appeared.

At dawn on Monday the 31st of May, Nasmith ordered diving stations, went to twenty feet, and headed for Panderma. It always pleased him to press home an attack on an enemy port: it was more effective, more demoralising, and if he sunk a ship, the crew would have a better chance to escape – he considered that the object of his patrol was to sink ships, not to drown seamen if it could be avoided. He also thought it was important that damage should be inflicted in full view of the inhabitants of a town, because it could not be concealed by any form of government censorship.

He coasted along the north shore of the Peninsula of Artaki, examining several bays among the cliffs and bold headlands where ships might shelter, but they contained only small sailing vessels which he did not stop to search, and fishing boats. He rounded Kapsala Burnu, where the cliffs end at the eastern point of the peninsula, and entered Peramo Bay, passing inshore of the scattered Mola Islands and their dangerous hidden reefs. At 8 a.m. he came in sight of Panderma, at the head of the bay – there was a single ship in the anchorage off the town, a large liner with two masts and one funnel.

"Liner bearing 210 degrees, at anchor. Distance five miles," he announced. There was tense excitement immediately. "Man the bow tubes."

He was astonished to see her there. How could the enemy have risked this great ship in an exposed roadstead? He carefully looked round for the patrols, but there were none. He moved in closer – there were no nets either. She didn't appear to be armed as far as he could discern. Perhaps in the emergency no defences had as yet been devised for Panderma, but it was strange that there were no protective measures of any kind.

"Flood bow tubes."

The town was pleasantly situated on a hillside overlooking the bay – quite a large town it seemed as they approached, with a great white mosque and pencil-thin minaret at its highest point. Beyond it, there was a gap in the mountains: that would be where the railway comes in from Smyrna.

On a slope outside the town to the right there was a very large military encampment, so there would be look-outs and perhaps artillery. Now he could see a number of small craft moving, plying backwards and forwards between the ship and the town, so she was evidently embarking troops. He couldn't have timed it better.

"Bow tubes ready, sir."

He set the torpedoes to run deep, so that they would do most damage to a ship of deep draught. He called D'Oyly and Brown to look at their victim through the periscope. Brown identified her as one of the latest ships of the German Rickmers Line.

She lay motionless and unsuspecting. Nasmith's only problem was how to do vital damage to his huge target without using more than one torpedo. He decided that a hit in the engine-room with its heavy machinery and large space with no watertight doors, would be the most deadly.

At 9.20 a.m. he got within range and fired the port bow tube. The torpedo struck the liner on the port side amidships and made an exceptionally loud report on exploding. She listed

132

heavily to port, showing the width of her decks with men on them running here and there. The small craft crowded round her to take the crew off. A tug came bustling out from Panderma, small puffs of smoke appearing in rapid succession on her funnel showed that she was hooting to attract the captain's attention. She passed under the bows of the ship and got a line on board. The ship slipped her anchors and the tug began to tow her towards the beach as she settled lower and lower in the water. Nasmith watched through his periscope. He could easily make sure of her with a second torpedo, but he had only three left. There was no doubt that she was very badly damaged, and that, even if she could be salvaged, it would take many months to repair her. He felt that he had done enough and that she wouldn't be of any further use to the enemy. He turned away and shaped course out of Panderma. When he was well clear of Peramo Bay, he surfaced to ventilate, and charge the batteries. The remainder of the day was spent patrolling to the north-east to intercept shipping coming along the southern coast of the Sea of Marmara, but nothing was sighted except a small tug making for Panderma.

The next task was to reconnoitre the Gulf of Ismid to find out if the port of Ismid, at the head of it, was also being used to embark troops as had been suggested in the signal they had received. It was a long, narrow gulf at the extreme eastern end of the Sea of Marmara, twenty-seven miles long, five across, but closing in at two points to little over a mile.

With the last of the daylight, E 11 dived to periscope depth and slipped into the entrance of the gulf between the high white cliffs of Yelken Kaya Burnu to the north, and the low rounded point of Chatal Burnu to the south. No enemy ships were sighted.

Night came on quickly, and when it was quite dark, Nasmith went close in to the northern shore near the ancient Byzantine castle of Eski Iskalese – half a mile beyond it, the main railway line to Aleppo and Baghdad from Scutari, opposite Constantinople on the Bosphorus, comes down close to the sea and follows the coastline for twenty-seven miles all along the Gulf of Ismid. It was the section D'Oyly had selected as the most suitable for his raid, and Nasmith had promised him an opportunity to survey it. They moved a little farther along the coast, surfaced four hundred yards from the beach, trimmed well down, stopped the motors and waited. Only Nasmith, D'Oyly and Brown were on the bridge. This point on the railway was

133

thirty miles from Scutari, nearly 600 miles by rail via Smyrna to Panderma, but only ninety miles from Panderma by sea.

The night was very still. They could hear the beat of horses' hooves, the creaking of a mill, dogs barking and yelping, the cackle of geese and hens in a suddenly disturbed farmyard, music and laughter as in a tavern – and at last the hoot of a train. It must have been far away, for it was a considerable time before they caught the chugging of the engine and rumble of heavy wagons approaching from the direction of Scutari. The sound faded as the train went round the shoulder of a hill, or through a tunnel, and then began again a much louder "jungle-jungle-jungle-jungle-jungle;" she was swinging along merrily now on the level. They strained their eyes, and were surprised to see nothing, the sound was so distinct – perhaps the train was in a cutting ... then they saw moving lights, higher than they expected, for the line ran along the top of a cliff. They had judged from the sound that it was a goods train, and now they could see it dimly: there was a white light on the funnel of the engine, a green light on the buffers and another white light looking forward from the guard's van that was higher than the trucks. "If only we had a gun!" Brown muttered. It was what all three were thinking. The sound abruptly changed its tone to a harmonious roar, showing that the train was crossing an iron bridge.

Nasmith counted the seconds aloud, "That is One that is Two that is Three ..." until it changed again. "It's a long bridge – a viaduct – quarter of a mile, I should say."

By the time the train had rumbled away, showing two red tail lights rapidly fading, another was approaching from the same direction, and far along the gulf they could see the lighted windows of a passenger train coming up from Ismid.

"This is obviously the place to land!" D'Oyly's voice was vibrant with excitement, but Nasmith wasn't going to be hurried.

"I'm not so sure. The cliffs are perhaps too steep for you to climb, especially in the dark. We'll have a look in the morning. What do you think, Brown?"

"I think, sir, he should land farther along by that farmyard. At least he could bring us back some eggs!"

D'Oyly laughed good-humouredly. "That's all you think of – food!"

"What water is there here, Brown?" Nasmith asked.

"Thirty-five fathoms, sir."

"Then we can't lie on the bottom. We'll try the new method again . . ."

He took the boat down, and again found the heavy density layer at seventy feet. When she wouldn't go down any farther he took in five tons of water ballast to keep her from coming up, then dismissed the men. They were told to turn in, except for the watchkeeper at the depth-gauge.

Alone with Nasmith for a few minutes in the wardroom, Brown suddenly asked, "You're not really going to let him try?"

Nasmith wasn't surprised at the question, for he had felt for some time that Brown had something on his mind. He answered firmly, "Certainly I'll let him try, if his plan sounds reasonable."

"He wouldn't have a chance, not one chance in a hundred, of getting back again. He's only twenty-three. Think what he might do with his life if he doesn't chuck it away. What's it all in aid of? To blow up a bit of line! Even if he could do it, it would be repaired again six hours later."

"That's true of course," Nasmith agreed, "but it would have tremendous repercussions. And I think he has a good chance of doing it, and of getting back again – otherwise I wouldn't let him try."

"Surely the railways and bridges will be guarded – they usually are in wartime, even in England. Can you imagine what we'll feel like waiting here, straining our ears, listening for a shout, a challenge, a shot – perhaps an explosion – that will give him away anyhow – then rifle fire, then . . . perhaps nothing. Nothing at all, ever again, and the awful decision of how long to wait . . . is he dead? Is he still alive?"

For some time Nasmith didn't speak, then he looked up and said very slowly, "I have thought of all this – many times."

Their eyes met, and Brown looked away. He had had a sudden insight into the nature of Nasmith's responsibilities. "I'm sorry," he muttered. "I won't mention it again. Must get a bit of shut-eye." He went and lay down on his bunk.

At 4 a.m., after listening in silence for possible enemy patrols, they blew the extra ballast (which sends a stream of bubbles to the surface) and went slow ahead on both motors. They rose to twenty feet. She was slightly down by the head. This was corrected as far as possible by adjusting the amount of water in the tanks, then the motors were stopped, the hydroplane wheels were set back to the zero mark, and D'Oyly distributed the men evenly through the boat. The last one was moved a pace or two backwards and forwards until the bubble in the spirit level was exactly in the centre. She gradually lost way and stopped. Even raising the periscope had to be compensated for by taking in slightly more ballast, but the result was a perfect, if precarious, static trim. The top of the periscope came out of the water causing no ripple on the glassy surface.

It was broad daylight, but the sun's rays had not yet reached the waters of the narrow gulf. They were exactly opposite the viaduct. D'Oyly, looking through the periscope, drew a sketch of it, noting its iron trellis work construction, and then made a sketch map of the track and as much of its surroundings as he could see. When he had finished, they retracted the periscope, went ahead on the motors, dead slow, and found that in these still waters the boat maintained her perfect trim without a touch on the hydroplane wheels – but it was tiring for the men as they were not allowed to move from their positions.

Ten minutes later Nasmith raised the periscope for another look. The scenery was most beautiful. Mountains with deep valleys rose steeply on both sides of the gulf, cultivated on the lower slopes with many villages and orchards, pasture above them with outcrops of rock and streaming waterfalls, and then dark pine forests reaching up towards an array of majestic snow-clad peaks. He felt an intense desire to be up there, to walk in the snow, to smell the pines, to drink the pure mountain water, and the foul air of his cramped quarters seemed by comparison ten times more foul. He concentrated firmly on the coastline and the railway. They followed it for some miles, trying to establish where the tracks lay closest to the water, and where the cliffs were low. They examined all the anchorages on the way up, but there were no troopships, nor any other ships except the usual small sailing vessels which they left unchallenged as they didn't want to betray their presence.

They left the gulf, still undetected, patrolled till nightfall, then surfaced, charged batteries, and headed for the signalling billet.

Nasmith took the first watch, from eight till midnight. They were running on the surface using the main engines, but he sent the helmsman to the steering position in the control room and dismissed the look-outs. Visibility was good, and he felt the need to be alone and silent on the bridge with all his troubles below him and the stars above. He had the gyro repeater compass before him, casting a faint glow, so he could see that the helmsman was steering the correct course, and he could pass orders to him through the voice-pipe. In emergency he had only to sound the klaxon and the men would be at their diving stations in a few moments, or he could call the messenger who waited in the control room immediately below the conning tower hatch. .

The pros and cons of D'Oyly's plan to blow up the railway weighed heavily on his mind. The viaduct seemed to be the most vulnerable place, but the most likely to be defended. In a small bay to the east of it, there was deep water right up to the rock-strewn shore, and he would be able to drop D'Oyly and his raft within a few yards of it. The cliffs on a moonless night would prevent the submarine being seen except by a watcher actually on the beach, or on the very edge of a cliff. The climb would be difficult in the dark with a heavy pack, and the return more difficult if he were closely pursued, but D'Oyly was strong and agile. The plan had a reasonable chance of success, and Nasmith felt that he would have to agree to it. It was inevitable that he, as captain, should get most of the credit for their joint exploits, but this, if all went well, would be a personal triumph for D'Oyly.

They reached the signalling billet without incident, and made contact with *Jed*. Nasmith's signals reported that no ships had been seen in the Gulf of Ismid, that there was a large military camp at Panderma and that he had torpedoed the Rickmers liner there. He himself was not convinced that the troops had come all the way from Constantinople by rail. He thought it more likely that they had come from Syria where, at the outbreak of hostilities, it was known that three Turkish army corps were stationed. Similarly, if any were sailing from Ismid, they could have come by train from Mosul or Baghdad. It seemed unlikely that Panderma would have been left as defenceless as he had found it, if it was intended to be the main embarkation point of the enemy's communications. The troops he had deprived of their transport would have a long march to Lampsaki on the Asiatic shores of the Dardanelles, to be ferried across to the town of Gallipoli.

The information he received from *Jed* was that convoys were again sailing from Constantinople.

TWELVE

At 4 a.m. on Wednesday the 2nd of June, E 11 unshipped the wireless masts, dived to twenty feet and patrolled to the north-east along the northern traffic route. The weather was fine with a light easterly wind.

At 8.10 it was reported to Nasmith that the smoke of a ship had been sighted astern. He went to the periscope and examined it carefully. After some minutes he was able to make out its approximate course. He surfaced and steered to intercept it. Visibility was good, and in another ten minutes he could distinguish her masts and funnel: then the form of the ship appeared. He could tell by her narrow beam and white bow wave that she was a small destroyer travelling at high speed. He had no intention of wasting one of his three precious torpedoes on a destroyer, unless in self-defence, so he decided to give her a wide berth. As he was about to dive, a patch of smoke was reported to the east. He went down to periscope depth. The smoke soon resolved itself into a large supply ship. He observed the two vessels approaching from opposite directions, and steered a course to intercept the supply ship when the destroyer would be too far off to interfere.

At 9 a.m. he surfaced. The destroyer was now nearly out of sight, but the supply ship was only three or four miles away. Twenty minutes under the full power of the diesels put him directly in her line of advance. She had two masts and one funnel, and was deeply laden. She was steering a straight course, and apparently relying on her speed to keep her out of trouble. He dived to twenty feet, manœuvred into position, and at 9.40 fired the starboard bow tube. The ship must have been laden with munitions. The torpedo struck her on the port side just before the bridge. The explosion was very violent, appearing to lift the whole of her upper deck overboard, and a heavy pall of smoke covered her. When the smoke cleared, her bows were already under the water, and in three minutes she had completely disappeared.

Nasmith handed the periscope over to Brown to continue the patrol, and went back to the wardroom. The crew had hailed his success with their usual shout of delight, and he had detected an added ring of excitement in their voices, as if they were feeling that, with only two torpedoes left, the long patrol would soon be over and they already had visions of leave and beer in Malta. The perils of the descent of the Straits affected them not at all – that was Nasmith's problem, not theirs. They had got up the Straits all right, so there was no reason why they shouldn't get down again – with the bit of luck that every submariner needs and which they now felt that Nasmith had. It was not at all certain, however, that E 11 would be recalled even when she had expended all her torpedoes: it would depend on whether Boyle in E 14 refitting in Malta was ready to relieve her. It was a pity that Commander Samson couldn't keep him supplied with torpedoes, but they were too heavy. The biggest bomb that the naval planes had yet carried weighed only 200 lbs. He had to console himself with the thought that even the presence of a submarine in the Marmara was a disturbing factor for the enemy. She would have to allow herself to be sighted frequently by the patrolling gunboats and destroyers and by the coast defences, she would have to stop and search caiques whose crews could be relied upon to spread the alarm when they got back to their villages: she would have to make a nuisance of herself in every possible way, by D'Oyly's raid on the railway, by stopping unescorted ships, boarding them and blowing them up with demolition charges as they had succeeded in doing in the case of *Nagara*. As long as E 11 was in the Marmara the enemy would be forced to delay and re-route his convoys and divert part of his war potential to defending his ships and harbours and the vulnerable sections of rail communications.

At 10.15 Brown reported that he had sighted a small steamer close inshore and had altered course towards her. When Nasmith got to the periscope, she had disappeared into a bay. Ten minutes later she appeared again, slipping round a headland – she was cautiously following the outline of the coast, keeping as near to it as she could. He stalked her patiently. At 10.50 a.m. he fired the port beam tube – and missed. The ship saw the track, turned at once and made for the shore. Nasmith surfaced and tried to head her off, but she put on an extra turn of speed and got away. It looked as if she was going to beach herself at the mouth of a little river near the small town of Panidos – it was a large village, really, surrounded by mills with smoking chimneys – but at the last moment she let go her anchor. The crew lowered a boat and hastily pulled for the shore.

Nasmith decided to put a demolition party aboard to blow her

139

up. As soon as he approached her, a volley of rifle fire rang out from the village. Bullets spattered on the water uncomfortably close, one ricocheting off the conning tower. It was obviously impossible to proceed with his plan. He left the ship and circled round looking for his torpedo which, like the others, had been set to float. There was no sign of it. Had it sunk after all, or run close inshore? Every time he went near the village, rifle fire broke out again. He reluctantly came to the conclusion that in face of this opposition he wouldn't be able to pick it up even if he found it. To avoid casualties, and to preserve his single periscope, he abandoned the search, headed out to sea and dived to twenty feet as soon as there was enough water.

He was disgusted at losing one of his two remaining torpedoes by this unexpected turn of events. It had never occurred to him when he launched the torpedo that he would be prevented by rifle fire from picking it up again. There must have been troops in the village, perhaps en route for the front from Rodosto ten miles up the coast. They never showed themselves, so it would have been impossible to return their fire with any effect, and there would have been no point in firing at random on the village. What annoyed him most was that the supply ship was not very large and he might not have expended a torpedo on her had he not felt sure that he would be able to pick it up again in the event of a miss.

In the light of what had happened, it was easy to see that he had made a mistake in tactics. Such a cautious captain might have been frightened into running for the shore if the submarine had surfaced, or even showed her periscope near him. Then he could have used his torpedo when the ship was at anchor, in spite of the rifle fire. He hadn't sufficiently considered the psychology of the captain, which was plain enough from his behaviour: that was the lesson he drew from the failure of this attack when he went over it again with D'Oyly and Brown. He accepted the fact that he had missed, though his private opinion was that the torpedo had not run true. As he wasn't sure, he didn't say so, because the torpedomen were always mercilessly derided by the rest of the crew if it was suspected that they had failed to make the proper adjustments.

Patrol was continued, and at 12.20 p.m. – they were well out to sea now – smoke was again sighted. Excitement ran high when it resolved itself into a ship escorted by two destroyers and it was realised that Nasmith considered it a target worthy of their last torpedo. She was small, two-funnelled, the type used for carrying despatches. She was moving fast, and the destroyers were being handled with their customary skill. It was because the enemy considered her to be worth protecting that Nasmith felt she was worth attacking.

The approach was difficult because, to press home his attack at close range, he had to get between the inshore destroyer and the ship without being observed. The wind had fallen, and the sea was so calm that the white wake of the periscope could easily be seen on the glassy surface. He lowered it when still 3.000 yards from the destroyer and navigated blind, listening to the propeller noises, estimating courses and distances, until he judged he was in the attacking position. When he raised it next, he was only six hundred yards from the ship. The bearing was on. He fired immediately and watched the track running straight for her bridge – but it was a miss under. Decidedly this was his off day. It was the torpedo that had failed to go off on hitting the refugee ship, so he knew it had a tendency to run deep, but he thought that the correct adjustments had been made. The despatch vessel must have been of very shallow draft.

The ship and the destroyers went straight on without any alteration in course. The attack had not even been observed. Nasmith waited impatiently for them to pass out of sight, for he was now without torpedoes, and it was essential to find this one again. He didn't want to lower his average by finishing up with two misses. It would be a bit of a let-down for the men too. Fortunately the idea recurred that this temperamental torpedo was destined to sink *Barbarossa* – he heard half-jocular prophecies to that effect which he was pleased to encourage. It wasn't such an impossible idea after all. They had seen *Barbarossa* heading for Gallipoli only six days earlier, and it was reasonable to suppose that she was still in the Straits and that they would have a chance to attack her on the way down.

The convoy disappeared, and they were able to surface and look for the torpedo. It wasn't very long before they found it, and the crew greeted it like an old friend. This time there was no bash on the nose – it had been a clean miss under.

Nasmith stopped the engines at a safe distance, D'Oyly looked at him inquiringly, got an answering nod, threw off his clothes and swam out to it with a spanner as Nasmith had done on the previous occasion. He really had no fear that D'Oyly would bungle it, but his first impulse was always to do

141

a job himself. He'd heard a grouse from the torpedomen also who thought it was their job: at least there was no lack of volunteers for any tricky work that had to be tackled.

While D'Oyly unscrewed the firing pistol, set it to "safe" and passed it aboard, Nasmith prepared to try out his new method of recovery. He trimmed the boat down by taking in ballast until she was exactly horizontal and the cap of the stern tube was awash. He ordered the tube to be flooded. Then, keeping the inner door of the tube closed, he ordered the cap to be swung open.

Six seamen dived into the water and, led by D'Oyly, they secured a steadying line to each side of the tail of the torpedo and guided its nose into the mouth of the stern tube. It was rocked gently and pulled forward until the lugs at the sides fitted squarely into the grooves.

The next order was: "Start the pump on the tube!" The leading torpedoman started the pump and as the tube emptied, the torpedo was sucked into it with a soft "Whoosh!" The outer cap was closed, the tube pumped dry, the inner door opened – and the torpedo was home again, but with the nose pointing inward. It was then drawn from the inner end of the tube, hoisted on a chain winch to the little trolley running on an overhead rail, which was used for transporting heavy weights, and guided by a working party right through the boat until it could be loaded into the port bow tube. Now it was the right way round and ready, after further inspection and adjustment, to be used for the third time. The whole operation had worked perfectly. The torpedo had been recovered in a fraction of the time, and with a fraction of the effort that it would have taken by the regular method, and without any risk to the submarine.

While the torpedo was being examined and tested, they turned away from the land and cruised about on the surface charging batteries. By the end of the day they were far out in the Marmara and had a very extensive view of the distant coastline to the northward. No ships appeared to be moving. When the batteries were charged, they dived, and for the third time found the heavy density layer at seventy feet – so it was probable that it extended over the whole of the Marmara at this depth. Nasmith's discovery of how to make use of it was of enormous benefit to the crew. The knowledge that they had only to dive to seventy feet and lie there expending no battery power except for lighting, filled them with confidence. They could sleep in perfect security. No one could find them, no weapon could touch them, they felt like kings. It was the "ormulu" – the gilded – way of obtaining rest, as Brown described it. During the whole night the depth on the gauge varied only four inches. They lay as securely as though they were lying on the bottom, but there was two thousand feet of water under their keel.

At daylight on the 3rd of June they surfaced and proceeded to a position south of Oxia Island. They had been so much in evidence the day before on the direct route from Constantinople to Gallipoli along the northern shore of the Marmara, that Nasmith thought the enemy ships might take a different route to-day, turning south on leaving Constantinople Harbour and going along the southern shore of the Marmara. The position he had chosen lay across that route.

It was even more probable that sailings had been suspended altogether after the sinking of the large ammunition ship and the attack on the small coaster, so it didn't seem necessary to patrol submerged. E 11 lay on the surface all morning charging batteries, the great precipitous mass of Oxia Island to the north, the widely scattered Princes Islands to the north and east with high mountain ranges beyond them. The men were bathing, cleaning ship and airing their sweat-soaked clothing in the sun, as no fresh water could be spared for washing them. The fresh water of the surface layer of the Marmara was brackish and wouldn't lather. They had all grown beards, some scraggy, some ferocious, except Nasmith who was, as always, clean shaven.

At 2 p.m. they dived and patrolled to westward. Nasmith was busy in the wardroom with D'Oyly, working on the "defect list," the table covered with books and miscellaneous forms and lists. Their patrol was already one of the longest on record, and he thought it possible that when he next contacted *Jed*, and reported that he had only one torpedo left, he would be ordered to return to Mudros. He hoped he would be, so that he could come back to the Marmara not only with a fresh supply of torpedoes, but with a gun and a good supply of ammunition. They would be sent to Malta for a refit. That meant that as soon as he got back to the parent ship he would have to present a list of the defects and the alterations required. Everything would be taken out of the boat and tested, but everything had first to be noted on a form in quadruplicate. Stores would be made up to establishment, or additional stores supplied, on forms pink or white under the correct headings. There were lists from the coxswain, the chief E.R.A., the L.T.O., the chief stoker ... there would be little time to worry about all this on the passage down the Straits. The engines would be stripped down, the batteries would require particular attention as they had regularly been run down too far and charged up again too quickly, the drinking water was a problem too – what was left tasted confoundedly of fuel oil – all the tanks would have to be tested for leaks. ...

Among the alterations, the most important was the fitting of a gun. They had not only to make out a strong case for having one, they had also to solve the technical problems involved as the gunnery people had discarded the idea as impracticable. That was why they were without one now. Nasmith, who in pre-war days had commanded the first submarine to be fitted with a gun, thought it was practicable, but it would naturally affect their trim and their underwater speed and, unless properly protected, might get caught up in anti-submarine nets or sweep wires. Where was it to be mounted? As near as possible to the conning tower hatch, of course, so that the gun-layer could nip out to it quickly when the boat surfaced – but before or abaft the conning tower? The plates might want strengthening to support a gun and withstand the shock of the recoil, and it might cause a leak in the firing tank below it ... and where was the ammunition locker to go? It would have to be on deck beside the gun, as every second would be precious. "I imagine an attack like this," Nasmith said, sketching as usual on a signal pad. "We'll have to wear our ensign while submerged: we can't fire without showing our colours and there won't be time to hoist them when we surface. It'll tear them to ribbons. Put down a couple of dozen ensigns on the demand note. ... I imagine an attack like this – at night, of course, on a rather slow moving target. We sight a ship ... here. We surface, say on her port quarter, coming up quickly to go down again quickly, get off three rounds – Bonk! Bonk! Bonk! – and dive. The ship's gunners won't have been able to get into action. Then surface somewhere else – starboard quarter this time – three rounds again, and dive. Then come up, perhaps right astern ... and go on like that till she's holed or set on fire ..."

Brown, who had the periscope watch, stepped into the wardroom: "Smoke to the north-east. Will you take a look, sir?"

Nasmith went to the periscope and studied the smudge on the horizon: "We'd better investigate ..." and he altered course towards it. "Up 200 revs. Let me know as soon as you can see what it is," and he went back to the wardroom.

Ten minutes later, Brown appeared again, "She's not getting any closer, sir."

Nasmith peered again at the smudge. It looked exactly the same as before. He ordered diving stations, brought the boat to the surface, switched over to the main diesel engines, and the chase began. The wind was north-east. A soft haze diffused the sun's rays so that the air glowed with light, the sea sparkled, the bow wave shone like a white flame, seabirds circled round them with shrill cries; it was good to be alive. Soon they could make out the form of the ship under the smoke. She was at an angle to their line of approach, so appeared foreshortened, but they could see she was not very large; she had clipper bows – she was something like a large steam yacht and the hull was painted white. She was not the sort of target Nasmith had in mind for his last torpedo, but he might perhaps stop her, order the captain to abandon ship, and sink her with a demolition charge. D'Oyly came up to have a look at her.

"She's altering course away, sir," Brown reported. "Must have sighted us."

She had narrowed to a blob on the horizon – they could now only see the width of the ship, and that with difficulty, because of the smoke that was pouring from her funnel.

"Can't you get a few more revs. out of the engines, D'Oyly?"

"I'll talk to the chief," D'Oyly said, and went below. Soon there was more vibration, and their speed increased by half a knot.

"We're overhauling her, sir."

Nasmith studied her again through his binoculars. She was definitely closer. He would have to be almost abreast of her to stop her with a rifle, but with a gun it would be simple. Yes ... with a gun, if only they would let him have one, and plenty of ammunition – he could get enough fresh water and provisions from captured sailing vessels and small steamers like this one – he would be prepared to maintain himself in the Marmara until the rest of the fleet got through and joined him. Then E 11 would lead them into Constantinople! That would be a proud day! It would knock Turkey out of the war, and then the Balkan countries ...

"We're closing her very fast, sir."

"What?" He looked again, and suddenly realised that she wasn't running away at all, but coming straight for them, the smoke in the following wind billowing ahead of her. He pressed the klaxons. "Diving stations!" The two ships were

145

racing towards each other, barely a mile apart. "Get below! Jump to it!" he shouted.

The helmsman banged down the lid of the magnetic compass and followed the look-out down the ladder. Brown grabbed up all the binoculars and the gyro repeater, and scrambled after them.

There was no report yet that all the vents were closed and it was safe for them to dive – impossible to wait: "Flood 1, 2, 3 and 4! Take her down! Fifty feet! Flood the auxiliary!" He shouted down the voice-pipe.

"Muffler valve's not closed, sir," came the agonised reply.

"Don't wait for it! Take her down! Quick!"

The coxswains, waiting quietly at the controls amid the feverish activity going on all round them, turned the hydroplane wheels. She settled lower and tilted forward. Nasmith dived for the hatch and banged it shut after him as a flurry of foam rushed over it and poured in, soaking him to the skin. He fastened the clips, shaking the water out of his eyes. Before he got down to the control room the ship thundered over them. He waited for the crash – it didn't come. The thrashing screw receded. . . .

"The muffler valve?" he asked.

"It's closed, sir, but the engine's full of water."

He felt like a man waking up from a deceitful dream. How could he have made such a mistake? Not notice the difference between a ship that was running away and a ship that was coming for them at a rate of knots? And not himself only – Brown, D'Oyly, the look-out? It was as if they had all been following a mirage.

"A record dive, sir!" Brown said cheerfully, showing him the stop-watch. "Sixteen seconds!"

The ship carried straight on. The sound of her throbbing faded away and didn't return. Now that the danger was past, the men were laughing and talking excitedly.

Nasmith ordered, "Bring her up to twenty feet," and then "Up periscope!" In the segment of blue light he saw the ship disappearing in the distance. He brought E 11 to the surface. She had to lie there while the stokers sweated at the laborious task of turning the main engines by hand – it needed two complete turns – to eject the water before they could be started again.

Half an hour later, a destroyer came in sight, zig-zagging at high speed, and evidently searching for them, so it seemed that

the ship had sent out a call for help. They dived, in a more dig-
nified style this time, stopped the engines and lay on the heavy
density layer at seventy feet.

THIRTEEN

At midnight Nasmith brought E 11 to the surface and set a
course for the signalling billet. They made contact with *Jed* at
3 a.m. on the fourth, reported the sinking of the large ammunition ship on the previous day, and that they had only one
torpedo left. They also asked for news of the land operations
but got no information.

At daylight they turned east once more and began to patrol
on the surface along the north coast of the Marmara, Nasmith
determined not to use his remaining torpedo unless a very
tempting target appeared. He was careful to discourage the
idea that they would be recalled. As he had to make as big a
nuisance of himself as possible, D'Oyly's proposed attack on
the Baghdad Railway seemed a good way to begin. There was
one other place where the railway approached the coast: this
was Kuchuk Chekmejeh Bay, on the north coast of the Marmara, only ten miles from Constantinople on the line to Uzun
Keupri and Adrianople. Nasmith thought it might be useful to
cause a diversion there as a possible alternative to the Gulf of
Ismid, so he decided to have a look at it.

They sighted nothing all that morning, but the smoke signals
at regular intervals told him that they had been spotted by the
shore watchers, which suited his purpose very well. When
Stephano Point came in sight, he turned away from the coast,
dived and went into Kuchuk Chekmejeh Bay at periscope
depth. He could see the railway, crossing several bridges over
small streams where it would be vulnerable; then it turned
inland, skirting a large lagoon. The main road from Constantinople to Rodosto crossed the mouth of the lagoon and continued along the coast. The railway ran along close to the coast
for two miles on the west side of Stephano Point. The only
advantage over the Gulf of Ismid project seemed to be that
there was not such a high cliff to scale. The disadvantages were
that so short a stretch of line so near the capital was likely to
be closely guarded, the bay gave no shelter from southerly winds

and, worst of all, the submarine, even on the surface, could not get within half a mile of the shore owing to shoal water, whereas in the Gulf of Ismid there was deep water right up to the base of the cliffs. D'Oyly agreed that the Gulf of Ismid offered him a better chance and, besides, the idea of blowing a hole in the famous Baghdad Railway appealed more strongly to his imagination.

Promising themselves that they would return to Kuchuk Chekmejeh when they had a gun, because they could bombard both main road and railway there, they continued their patrol on the surface across the approaches to Constantinople Harbour. D'Oyly overhauled his gear and prepared his raft to be ready for his attempt on the morrow. The fuse for the demolition charge had to be fired by a pistol which unfortunately made a loud report, and he tried several devices for silencing it without much success. Off Oxia Island they were forced to dive by a hostile destroyer.

When they came up in the evening, the same destroyer was still persistently hunting for them, so they went down to the seventy foot level and stopped the motors.

During the night, the situation was radically and unexpectedly changed, D'Oyly's project had to be abandoned and all Nasmith's thoughts had to be devoted to the problem of mere survival. The E.R.A.s inspecting the engines found a crack in the starboard intermediate shaft – the shaft between the engine and the electric motor. It was the same defect which had delayed them at Malta on the way out. It meant that when they were using the diesels the shaft might break at any time, particularly if they put any additional strain on it by increasing speed suddenly. Meanwhile, the electricians testing the insulation of the armature discovered a full brilliancy earth on the port motor. They were constantly testing the insulation by putting a lead with a light in it from the armature to the hull of the boat, and if the light came on brilliantly it indicated a serious leak and it was called "full brilliancy." It meant that the armature couldn't be used without risking a flash or a fire and the complete wrecking of the motor. It was impossible to repair either of these defects with the means at their disposal so E 11, from being a first-class fighting unit, was all at once a crock in urgent need of dockyard assistance: and the hazardous return passage of the Straits became a very serious prospect.

They spent the following day cleaning and ventilating the boat, bathing, and topping up the batteries. During the afternoon they made their way on the surface to the signalling billet. Instead of passing their signals between midnight and 3 a.m. as they usually did, they established communication with *Jed* at 8 p.m. and asked permission to return. By daylight they had had no reply, so they made for the centre of the Marmara and lay on the surface while Nasmith and D'Oyly made a complete inspection of the boat. Nasmith didn't imagine that the Turks had neglected to improve their defences in the Straits during the past month. They knew that there was a submarine in the Marmara, that sooner or later it would have to return to its base, and that the Narrows would be the best place to catch it. Also, it was vitally important to them to prevent any more submarines repeating their exploit and continuing the havoc wrought on their shipping by E 11 and E 14 before her. He thought it possible that the Straits could be effectively sealed by nets, which were of two kinds, the most dangerous being a loose trailing net designed to envelope a submarine and foul her propellers. It was usually fitted with explosive charges and with floating buoys which betrayed any movement of the submarine to watchers in surface craft. The other kind was a rigid net of 2½ or 3 inch steel wire, through which Nasmith hoped to crash at full speed – but their full speed was now reduced from eleven knots to about six knots when submerged. He had information, before he began the patrol, that a net was being constructed, but he did not know if it had been completed, and he could only guess at its nature and the best way to penetrate it. He thought it probable that more mines had been laid, for there had now been ample time for the Turks to get a fresh supply from Germany, rail communications being open through Bulgaria. There was little he could do to provide against these hazards, except to make sure that all external fittings were properly protected by guards and jumping wires to prevent them as far as possible from fouling any obstruction.

He could see that D'Oyly, who had been keyed up for his raid on the Baghdad Railway, was bitterly disappointed. It was useless even to discuss the possibility of carrying on with it. They both realised that with defective engines which might let them down at any moment, the risk would be unjustifiable. Their business now was to get the boat home and into the repair yard as soon as possible.

When it got dark, at 9.30 p.m. on the sixth, they started for home. The men were rested, the batteries were topped up, and everything was in as good order as they could make it. D'Oyly

149

had carefully adjusted the ballast to compensate for the food, water and fuel consumed, and for the torpedoes expended. As soon as they got within range of *Jed* they stopped, rigged the wireless aerial, and tried to communicate with her, Nasmith hoping that the signal recalling them would come through. As the set behaved even worse than usual, and it was soon apparent that they were unlikely to receive any decipherable signal, he told the wireless operator to signal their ETA, Expected Time of Arrival, off Cape Helles at noon on the following day. It was most important that this should be known and that a destroyer should be sent to meet them. If they surfaced unexpectedly in the British controlled area they stood a good chance of being sunk by their own patrols without being given an opportunity to identify themselves, for the warships using their guns to support the land operations were menaced by U Boat attack. It took more than an hour to get this short signal through, the aerial sparking badly all the time, and threatening to give away their position. Next he tried to obtain information about the two enemy battleships, *Barbarossa* and *Turgut Reiss,* for he had not abandoned his intention of attacking them if they were still in the Straits.

At 3.40 a.m. dawn was breaking, and they had received nothing from *Jed*, not even the acknowledgment of their ETA signal. They unshipped the aerial and wireless masts, dived to twenty feet, and headed for the entrance to the Straits. The forest-clad mountains of Asia Minor gradually closed in on them on one side, and the rough, yellow hills of the Gallipoli Peninsula on the other. They had only forty-seven miles to go, and in spite of the dangers ahead, the men were cheerful and Nasmith was confident. In place of the glassy calm he so much dreaded, a freshening wind from the north-east whipped up the surface of the water – if it held, it would prevent his periscope from being easily seen, and this time the current, to a depth of about thirty feet, was in his favour.

At 9.30., with only 33 miles to go, he dived to ninety feet to pass under the Gallipoli minefield. This was negotiated successfully, and he came up again to twenty feet to begin his hunt for the battleships. In the first bay on the Asiatic side there were only small steamers and dhows lying off the port of Lampsaki where the road from Panderma reaches the Straits. He moved over to the European side and examined the anchorage at Karakova – it was empty. Back to the Asiatic side to Umurbey Iskelesi, but there were still no battleships. The idea that their one remaining torpedo, which had been twice fired already and twice recovered, was destined to sink the *Barbarossa* had completely taken possession of the crew, and every time they approached a new anchorage and Nasmith examined it through the periscope, they expected to hear she was in sight.

As they approached Moussa Bank, they sighted a large liner, evidently an empty transport. She was lying at anchor, an easy target. Nasmith was tempted to sink her – but what if *Barbarossa* was farther down? It would be exasperating to get within striking distance of her at last, with empty tubes. She had been saved once by the dazzling rays of the sun, and again by the brightness of the moon; would she be saved again by the accident of the empty transport drawing their last torpedo? The men were closed up for action, the tube ready. He passed within three hundred yards of her, he watched her come into his sights – but he restrained the impulse to fire.

When he came to Nagara Point with its treacherous shoals he went well over to the European side and got a clear view through the periscope of the whole of the next reach as far as Chanak. It was empty. There was no sign of a battleship. He knew they would not be farther down, for it was from here that they could most conveniently bombard Anzac Beach, lobbing sixteen-inch shells across the Peninsula.

He had already made up his mind what to do if *Barbarossa* didn't appear. Without a word of explanation to his crew, he dived to fifty feet, flooding the auxiliary to pass through the critical level between the densities, and reached the up-flowing seawater. Then, instead of turning 90 degrees to go on round the point, he turned 180 degrees and headed up the Straits again – it was a difficult manoeuvre as the channel was only a mile across and E 11, like all her class, had a wide turning circle: he had to increase the revolutions to full ahead on the starboard motor to get her round. He ignored D'Oyly's quizzically raised eyebrow and the blank faces of the crew who were astounded to find themselves heading for the Marmara again. He met strong cross currents which set him in towards Akbas Limani, but he used the periscope as infrequently as possible, keeping it up each time for only a few seconds, for of course it threw up more spray going against the surface current than on the way down. The defective motor was running hot, but at noon he was within striking distance again of the transport off Moussa Bank. She was lying to the stream and showing her broadside. When he got level with her, he rose to twenty feet and turned to starboard to bring the bow tubes to bear. If only the temperamental torpedo would run true, nothing could save her now except the appearance of *Barbarossa* – and *Barbarossa* did not appear. Once more he watched the great ship come into his sights at a distance of only 300 yards. He fired the port bow tube. This time the torpedo ran true. It struck her on the port side forward with a tremendous crash. She immediately heeled over to port and began to settle by the head. He continued his turn to starboard and went on down the Straits leaving the transport sinking behind him. This made a total score for the patrol of five large steamers, two small steamers and a gunboat.

He safely negotiated Nagara Point, giving it a fairly wide berth, but off Kilid Bahr E 11's trim became quite abnormal, as if the ghost were getting hold of her again. He was trying to force her bows down, flooding the forward trim, when she suddenly took an angle by the stern, then jerked her bows up and down again. To prevent her breaking surface he did what he had done off Heligoland – he hastily flooded the interior ballast tanks and managed to hold her and force her down to seventy feet on a more or less even keel with eight tons of additional ballast. The currents were swinging her in all directions and they were heading straight for the European shore when there was a harsh scraping sound: the boat listed and swung to port. He glanced at Brown, "What water is there?"

"Thirty-five fathoms, sir," Brown replied promptly. It confirmed his own estimate. The depth-gauge read 75 feet: they couldn't possibly be aground, and yet it felt like it.

"She wants to go off to port, sir," the helmsman reported. "Carrying five degrees of helm, sir."

Perhaps they had fouled a piece of wreckage ... Better go up and have a look. "Twenty feet," he ordered.

"She's heavy, sir," the coxswain reported.

"We must get her up. Put two men on the forward hydroplane wheel."

The men strained at the big wheel. She rose slowly and levelled off at twenty feet. He called for silence, and listened for propellers ... there was no sound. "Up periscope – slowly ... that's enough." He looked through the lens.

The men were silent, looking at him and wondering what had happened; wondering also why he didn't immediately order "Down periscope" again, but he couldn't possibly tell them what met his horrified gaze: at first glance he thought it was a rock, a round black object with trailing seaweed only twenty feet from the lens – but it was moving with them and kicking up the spray. It was a large horned mine they were dragging along with them. They must have fouled its moorings. He straightened up and carefully wiped the eye-piece with the chamois leather to give himself time to face the crew. He felt that Wheeler, who was always beside him at the periscope and studied his expressions, already suspected that something was wrong. His first instinct was to surface and try to clear the mine, but they were right under the batteries of quick-firing guns defending the Narrows, so that would be suicide. He would have to make up his mind quickly, for the mine was making a tremendous wash and betraying their presence. He saw that he would have to dive again, carrying the mine down with him.

D'Oyly, seeing that he had not retracted the periscope, stepped up to him, "Can I have a look, sir?"

Nasmith replied casually, "Not just now, D'Oyly," and turned to Wheeler: "Down periscope."

In that instant he had decided to handle the situation entirely by himself. He alone knew they were facing imminent death. When it came it would be quick, but he could spare them the agony of waiting for it. There was no point at all in letting the crew know, for they could do nothing about it, and the slightest nervousness or excitement among them would make his own task more difficult. Of course they were wondering what had happened, but nothing they could imagine would be worse than the reality. He couldn't tell D'Oyly or Brown without the others hearing also, or at least without them realising that something was seriously amiss. "I'm going to take her down again," he said. "We're off Chanak."

Brown marked the position on the chart, and added, "Course 220 degrees. Time 1 p.m."

"Right. Take her down to thirty feet – slowly, and don't dip below thirty, or we'll be in a counter-current. Steer 220 degrees."

He unclipped the lower conning tower hatch, climbed into the conning tower, opened one of the deadlights and looked out through the thick glass scuttle into the green translucent water to see how the mine would behave when they dragged it under. He looked up and saw the shining roof of the surface and the black blob of the mine surrounded by a dark stream of disturbed water. He could see the shadowy mooring wire also, connecting the mine to the submarine – it had fouled the port hydroplane but without taking a turn round it, and was held in place only by the forward movement of the boat and because the weight of the sinker hanging beneath was equal to the drag of the mine above. If the wire slipped downwards it would pull the mine down on to the foredeck: if the wire slipped upwards the mine would be washed against the conning tower – it was a perfect balance. The bows were dipping now ... The water cleared as the mine was pulled under. It surged from side to side and swung down towards the conning tower ... It was only ten feet from the scuttle through which he was looking. He counted six horns sticking out of it. They were made of lead, each one covering a glass tube. On contact with the hull of the submarine, the soft leaden horn would crumple, the glass tube within it would break, releasing acid which would complete the electric circuit to the detonator, firing the charge. He could see a circular plate surrounded by small bolts – it covered the detonator. There would be a flash of fire and the charge of eighty pounds of high explosive would tear away the three-quarter-inch steel plating of the hull as easily as if it were made of paper. Even the slight upward movement of a flexible sleeve on the mooring wire could detonate it. How was he going to get rid of the thing? With her crippled motor the boat would take about three hours to get clear of the Straits and out of the range of the batteries. He mustn't make a mistake now. D'Oyly's fertile imagination would lead him to make ingenious suggestions of what ought to be done, but he mustn't allow anyone to distract his attention with advice. It was the supreme test for which all his past training and experience had been preparing him. The knowledge that he must face it alone gave him strength. He had passed so many nights on the bridge alone with the stars, that he felt it was right that he should be alone now without human aid in the crisis of his life. He felt a kind of exhilaration as the boat dipped farther and the mine surged towards him. It no longer mattered whether he had been a good skipper or a rotten skipper, he had done his best and he was content to let it go at that. He could tell by the increasing darkness of the water that they were going too deep. "Hold her at thirty!" he shouted down to the coxswain. "Two men on the wheel! Don't let her go below thirty!" He had a momentary vision of the interior of a submarine they had salvaged in the North Sea after she had hit a mine. His men had served him well. He didn't want them to die like that – particularly D'Oyly. Through all their association, through the strain of events and of being always in each other's company, there had never been the slightest ill-feeling between them. It must have been because of some special quality in D'Oyly's character: he would have liked to thank him, for he knew that he owed him much. What was it? A quality of generosity? Of loyalty? Of tranquillity? That was it. A certain tranquillity that made him accept with equal good humour whatever came along. The mine remained a few feet away from the conning tower, the mooring wire slanting back from the port hydroplane at an angle of about thirty degrees. The slightest swirl of the current or movement of the hydroplane might cause it to slip those crucial few feet.

"Kephez should be abeam, sir," Brown's voice reached him.

"Very good," he answered mechanically. They were approaching the minefield. He would have to go deep to pass under it.

He closed the scuttle, went down the steel ladder with slow deliberate steps, and took up his accustomed position among the men in the control room. He signed to a stoker to close the lower hatch, shutting off the conning tower. All along the boat the men at their diving stations were looking at him, but he took no notice. Only Dowell at the hydroplane wheel remained impassive, his eyes fixed on the depth-gauge, Brown was writing up his log, and there was an awareness in D'Oyly's attitude that action of some kind might be required of him at any moment.

Nasmith turned to the coxswains. "I want a very steady, regular dive – understand?"

"Ay, ay, sir."

"Right." He plunged his hands deep into his trousers pockets. "Eighty feet! Take her down!"

"Eighty feet, sir."

"Flood the auxiliary." They wouldn't get her down without extra ballast. The water hissed and roared in the tanks. He saw nothing of his surroundings, only the mine following them deeper into the green darkness and murky depths.

"Eighty feet, sir."

"Very good. Stop flooding. Steer two hundred and forty-eight degrees."

"Two hundred and forty-eight degrees, sir."

They had made a perfect dive, and now all waited in silence for the rasping sounds against the hull to begin. Nasmith shuddered inwardly as the first wire touched them and he knew that his mine was surging through the moorings of the other mines. He was thankful he hadn't shared his secret: to have terror in his own heart was enough. The hollow rapping, the ominous

155

scraping along the side, the quick orders to stop port, or stop starboard in case the propellers should foul the wires, continued – he couldn't tell how long. At last there was silence and he heard Brown's cheerful voice, "I think we're through, sir."

He hesitated to give the order to come up to thirty feet, to risk moving the hydroplane again that was holding the wire, but he would have to come up sometime. Better now, and get the benefit of the favourable current. He brought her up, but every time the hydroplane wheel was moved he could almost feel the mooring wire slipping inch by inch and the mine creeping nearer and nearer to the conning tower, but the minutes went by and nothing happened. The patent log clicked up another mile.

At 3.50 p.m. they were opposite the front line trenches. They altered course to make Cape Helles, at the seaward end of the Gallipoli Peninsula. As they crossed Morto Bay Nasmith called for silence, and they heard distant propellers, the sound that for three weeks had meant "enemies" and now meant "friends," but these friends would be as dangerous as enemies if the ETA signal had not got through. The nearest were recognisably drifters and M.T.B.s, so Nasmith passed quietly between them, and felt his way by dead reckoning along the coast until he heard the beat of a destroyer's propellers patrolling slowly up and down. When he had made sure of her position and the direction in which she was moving, for it would have been the end of both of them if the destroyer had passed over them and struck the mine, he risked putting the periscope up a few inches above the surface while she was heading away from him. Half a mile to starboard he saw the white cliffs of Cape Helles and the crowded beach below them with the landing ship *River Clyde,* busily discharging stores from lighters – and a new landmark, the keel and forefoot of a capsized battleship. The destroyer was half a mile to port. He identified her with relief as *Grampus,* of the same flotilla as *Grasshopper* who had escorted them in, so there was a good chance that she had been sent to meet them. Even as he watched, he knew that the look-out had spotted the periscope, for *Grampus* put her helm over to turn towards him. Had she been warned, he wondered, or would she assume that he was a U Boat and come in at full speed to ram? It would be a spectacular end to the patrol, destroyer, mine and submarine going up together in one colossal bang. The thought of D'Oyly's decoy periscope with a mine under it flashed uneasily across his mind. He'd have to surface at once and identify

156

himself, and surface without letting the mine touch the boat. . . .

He told Plowman to get up into the conning tower with an ensign to be ready to go out and hoist it, and sent for D'Oyly.

Plowman came clattering down the ladder again. He'd opened the scuttle – as he usually did to let some light into the conning tower – and looked out . . . "Sir!" he gasped, "There's a great big ball on the foredeck!"

"I know all about that," said Nasmith laughing. "It's a mine. It's not on the foredeck, fortunately for us, but floating above it." He turned to D'Oyly who was entering the control room, and spoke in a voice they could all hear, "We've fouled a mine forward, and we're going to get rid of it by going full astern and blowing the after tanks to keep her bows submerged. Tell them to disregard the defective armature, and give us all she's got."

"Stand by the blows!" said D'Oyly – he seemed to take it as a perfectly ordinary manœuvre – and they all went to their stations.

"Blow the after trim! Blow 5 and 6. Stop both! Full astern both!" He sent Plowman up into the conning tower again. The stern rose and the boat trembled as the reversing screws checked her way and sent a rush of water forward which swept the mine out over the bows – it hung there while the boat gathered stern way, then the mooring wire slipped off the hydroplane. The mine bobbed for a moment, then was dragged down by its sinker and disappeared.

When Plowman reported that the mine had gone, they continued going astern to get well clear, then blew the main ballast – and the whole length of the superstructure appeared above the surface. They hoisted the white ensign, and made a signal to *Grampus* that they had cleared a mine which had fallen into the sea ahead of them.

Grampus replied with three rousing cheers which were taken up and repeated by troops on the crowded decks of a passing trawler, and echoed by hundreds more on the beach who ran down to the water's edge shouting and waving their caps, ignoring a couple of shells which banged into the sea between them and the submarine.

Nasmith crowded as many of his men on to the bridge as it would hold, and called for three cheers for *Grampus,* to return the compliment.

While they changed over to the diesels, *Grampus* laid a dann buoy – a spar with a flag on it and a weight attached to a long wire to anchor it – to mark the spot where the mine was last seen, and called up the minesweepers to deal with it. Then she turned and led the way towards Kephalo.

E 11 followed, her wet hull glistening in the bright sun. Black smoke poured from her exhaust pipe aft, gradually thinning as the engines warmed up. Distant Samothrace lay like a blue cloud on the horizon. Cheers were still echoing from the cliffs of Helles, for it had spread like wildfire in the British lines that the fabulous E 11, whose exploits had been read to the troops in daily bulletins, had returned safely.

EPILOGUE

The Authors are happy to record that E 11 survived two more patrols in the Sea of Marmara in the course of which she sank a large number of Turkish vessels including the battleship *Barbarossa*.

There were further Allied losses, E 7 was caught in a net and destroyed by her crew, E 20 was ambushed at a rendezvous and torpedoed by a U Boat, and the French lost *Mariette* and *Turquoise*: but after E 11's first patrol the submarines kept the initiative.

Lieutenant-Commander Nasmith was awarded the V.C. and promoted. He subsequently commanded *Iron Duke,* then became an Admiral and held high commands in World War II. As Second Sea Lord he had the unusual experience of presenting the Dirk for the Cadet of the Year to his eldest son at the Royal Naval College, Dartmouth.

Lieutenant D'Oyly-Hughes built another raft and duly blew a hole in the Baghdad Railway – an early example of a successful commando raid. He was lost in World War II in the aircraft-carrier *Glorious,* of which he was in command, off the coast of Norway.

Lieutenant Brown returned to the Merchant Navy. Cock Dowell took his pension and was employed by the Science Museum rigging model sailing ships. Fore-end man Clark drove a London taxi.

Raymond Gram Swing got his story after the war, over a pleasant lunch with Nasmith at the United Services Club in London. He never resented the loss of his boots, typewriter and medicine chest: on the contrary, he was one of Britain's staunchest supporters in the dark hours of 1940. His heartening broadcasts, relayed across the Atlantic, will not quickly be forgotten.